Dixieland Murder

A Lucy DelRose Mystery

Teresa Lynn

DIXIELAND MURDER: A Lucy DelRose Mystery by Teresa Lynn

Copyright©2013 by Teresa Lynn

Cover design and interior formatting by Ellie Searl, Publishista®
www.publishista.com

ISBN-13: 978-0615873305
ISBN-10: 0615873308
LCCN: 2013948799

Printed in the United States of America

Black Bayou Publishing
Vicksburg, Mississippi

OTHER WORKS BY TERESA LYNN

THE LUCY DELROSE MYSTERIES

RIVER RAT

BO HACHE MYSTERIES

TO DISMISS WITH PREJUDICE

AWARD WINNING SHORT STORIES

"Faded Around the Edges"

"Partner"

"Blue Ribbon"

AWARD WINNING ONE-ACT PLAYS

"The Anniversary"

"What's Wrong with Harry?"

For Mom,
who had the wisdom to place the first romance novel
into the hands of a bored teenager
on a long, hot summer day.

CHAPTER ONE

"MISS LUCY, YOU GONNA PLAY with that fish or bring him in?" Mr. Wilkes leaned over the side of my runabout, the *Little Mermaid*. A grappling hook dangled from his hand.

"Mr. Wilkes, I grabbed a nice one, yeah?" I sputtered around a mouthful of water, fighting the catfish I held, his mouth seized in my gloved hand.

"Bring him over before you both go back under," he commanded me.

Sweet Mr. Wilkes, he had my back as my employee and friend. I struggled to get closer to the runabout, wading through clogs of grass and sediment.

Suddenly my feet were pulled out from under me. The catfish and I went back underwater and then *poof* my fish was gone. Something had a grip on my right ankle. Kicking I tore free of my attacker and surfaced, sucking air like a thirsty drunk. Moving closer to the grassy bank, I gained purchase against the sandy riverbed before screaming bloody murder, ready to fight whoever played a prank on me. Husky laughter broke through my fury. I blinked twice before the image of Rene Caron swam before my bleary eyes. His wet black hair snaked out about his shoulders as he treaded water. *Arrogant man*, I seethed. I punished him with both my fists pounding his chest. The water lapped against us.

"What the hell you think you're doing, Rene?" I yelled at him. I heard Mr. Wilkes chuckling in the background.

"Little mermaid, you're not supposed to be grabbling on your own," Rene whispered into my ear and then pulled me tight against his body.

I felt every inch of him pressing against me in the afternoon heat. The cool water had no effect on my overheated emotions. Rene was six foot two inches of pure testosterone and strong as an ox. His bronze chest was bare, and I had one hell of a time keeping my temper about me and not surrendering to him.

"What are you talking about? Mr. Wilkes is with me." I pushed against him, not wanting to lose this argument due to raging hormones. My fingers tightened against his chest and I felt the rippling of biceps. Rene was so damned sexy with those dark brown eyes looking down at me through long black lashes. His dark hair clung to his head and trailed down the back of his neck. I itch to stroke the wet strands.

"No, Lucy." His lips moved against my parted lips. "Mr. Wilkes is supposed to be *in* the water with you." He grabbed a handful of my tangled hair, pulled my head back, and pressed a kiss of ownership upon my mouth.

Embracing, we floated away from the bank and sank in a pool of sunlight. His large hand slipped down my body, pressing me tighter against him. His fingers eased between my thighs and caressed the throbbing ache inside me. I felt along the waistband of his jeans. I cursed my weakness; the man was driving me crazy. I accidentally gulped water and came up sputtering and coughing.

"Rene, no need to drown her," Mr. Wilkes scolded him sharply. He fired up the outboard motor and brought the runabout closer to shore.

"Now, Mr. Wilkes, I wouldn't hurt your boss," Rene said with a chuckle. He heaved me out of the water and into the runabout. "I don't want to catch her grabbling alone again."

"Rene Caron, just who the hell do you think you are, telling me what to do?" I growled at him. I was waterlogged, grouchy, and mad as hell for losing that forty-pound flat-head catfish because of his shenanigans. I brushed by waist-length hair back from my face.

"You *know* who I am, little mermaid." He winked at me and then turned away from us, swimming upriver toward his cruiser anchored in deeper water.

I had been so engrossed in the job at hand I hadn't noticed the ripple of waves at his arrival. Lucy DelRose, you need to get a grip, I told myself. I flopped down into the bow of the boat and Mr. Wilkes handed me a towel to wipe my face. I watched Rene's thirty-footer head downriver. He gave me a blare on his horn, but I looked the other way, ignoring his ornery ass. I swore I could hear his laughter as he motored past. Just because l was attracted to the man didn't mean he owned me. I could still feel the pressure of his lips against mine. I liked the way his callused hands touched me. Goosebumps spread along my arm, evidence of my fantasies.

Mr. Wilkes settled in the pilot seat and trimmed down the motor. We entered the main channel, making our way upriver to DelRose Marina Dock. Magnolia trees in full bloom graced the sloping hills with their perfumed white flowers. A swarm of buffalo gnats attacked us. Mr. Wilkes shoved the throttle up and sent us flying over the white caps to escape the onslaught of flesh eaters. We settled back to a normal speed and sailed through a cold spot in the river where the air was like a quick dip inside a refrigerator.

Miss Queen's, diesel motors rumbled past us as she headed downriver to the Port of New Orleans to unload her barges bearing grain. Captain Hayes waved to us from the pilothouse and gave a blast on his horn. I waved back, giving him thumbs up, and he returned the gesture. We were old high school buddies and always used this signal. His dark beard and curly hair made a nice combination for a riverboat pilot.

The floating marina came into view around the bend. It was held fast by two strong iron chains buried deep into rich riverbank soil. We rode in on our own wake to the dockside slip. Mr. Wilkes leaned over me and pressed the button to lift the boat from the river. His pink ears, speckled with brown freckles, shone delicate in the glare of the sun. Mr. Wilkes was like a tootsie roll — dark skin wrapped around a six foot frame. I dumped the cooler and fishing gear onto the dock before squishing my way toward the dock house. Mr. Wilkes followed, pulling the cooler.

"Lucy," Gran called out. At ninety-one years young, she was eternally beautiful. A butterfly comb secured her braided white hair. She wore a summer blue cotton shift that matched the color of her eyes, and white sandals cushioned her slender feet.

"Yes, Gran, coming," I mumbled, still grouchy. My hand burned like hellfire from the sharp teeth of the catfish. He left his mark on me, just like that half-breed Indian, Rene Caron. Wouldn't I just love to bite *him* all over.

"Oh, Lucy, you're hopeless," I moaned to myself.

"Mercy, child, who are you talking to?" Gran shaded her eyes with the back of her hand and gave me a worried look.

"It's nothing, Gran." I kissed her velvet cheek. The dock swayed as a boater motored too close to the marina. We suffered his backwash.

"Mommy," my son, Joey, called out to me from the dock house. I loved the sound of his voice.

"Out here, Joey," I said. His blond head appeared around the screen door.

"Did you grab a flat-head?" He was eager to hear about my dangerous escapades.

"Joey, I need to talk with your Mommy, honey. Can you clean the tables for me? " Gran smiled at him.

"Okay, Gran." My seven-year-old obliged his grandmother.

"I'll talk to you in a minute, sweetie," I yelled out to Joey.

"Lucy, honey—" Gran paused and seemed to wrestle with her inner thoughts. "Sue Ann Dykes is dead."

I couldn't have been more surprised if Gran had suddenly dived into the Mississippi River.

"How?" I asked, dumbfounded. Sue Ann and Junior Dykes were like family. I fought back the tears that threatened to flow.

"Someone killed her." Gran laid a hand on my damp sleeve and gave it a reassuring squeeze.

"My God," I said. Junior had to be going through hell. Sue Ann and Junior had had their problems of late, but they also had three adorable sons.

"Lucy, the sheriff's department is questioning Junior. They seem to think he knows something about her death," Gran ended in a whisper.

I gripped her arm. Junior was an old boyfriend who dropped me in our senior year to go with the head cheerleader.

Sue Ann had been the head cheerleader.

CHAPTER TWO

*C*OPE *COUNTY DEPUTIES ARE INVESTIGATING the homicide of Sue Ann Dykes, found dead in the front seat of her truck late Sunday evening. A motorist saw Dykes slumped over the steering wheel of her late model Chevrolet pickup truck and called 911. The medical examiner found knife wounds to her chest and lacerations about her neck. The coroner will perform an autopsy in Jackson late this afternoon to determine the exact cause of death. Dykes was the wife of nine years to Mack Dykes, Jr., and mother of three young boys.*

I put down the newspaper, my hands shaking. Sue Ann was murdered. It was too crazy to think about. Back in college, Sue Ann was a classic blonde-haired beauty. Time and three pregnancies had added a few pounds to her once shapely figure.

"Lucy, what does the paper say about Sue Ann?" Gran came into the kitchen from the back porch.

"Not too much, Gran," I said and folded the newspaper to the article for her to read.

I walked over to the stainless steel kitchen sink to fill a kettle with water. I dressed in fresh jeans and T-shirt after washing and drying my hair. I'd braided it to the side of my head so that the heavy braid fell over my breast and secured the end with a blue silk ribbon Rene had given to me a few days ago. I fondled the ribbon, remembering Rene's hand resting against my breast when he tied it around the braid, then pulled my thoughts back to the present. Sue Ann's killer was out there somewhere. This worried me. I could not believe Junior had anything to do with his wife's death.

I opened the canister that contained the tea bags and took five bags out. The kitchen wrapped me with its warmth and old-fashioned charm. The red brick floors were in their natural clay state. Cedar cabinets lined the walls, and stainless steel appliances made housework a little easier. The counters gleam deep green marble. A large rectangle island gave us more elbow room to cook, and a deep pit was built into the floor to hold charcoal that could heat a heavy black kettle cradled by an iron bar. The tea kettle whistled for my attention. I poured the hot water into the tea pitcher.

Mr. Wilkes knocked on the screen door before entering. He carried a tub of filleted catfish for tonight's supper. Joey trotted after him, toting a box of toys he had taken down to the dock house.

"Mommy, what's for lunch? I'm starved," Joey announced in a loud voice. His blond hair shone like a beacon.

"I've got pizza in the oven," I said and flipped on the oven light to check the progress of the bubbling cheese. "Just about done." I flicked the light off.

Gran threw the newspaper down on the table. "What *is* this world coming to?" she muttered.

"What's wrong, Gran?" Joey said with a worried look.

"Nothing, dear. Go on and put your toys away." Gran scooted back in her chair. "I'll set the table."

I followed Joey to his bedroom and helped him change into clean clothes.

"Gran's been upset all morning." Joey wiped his face with a towel. "She's been talking on the phone a lot."

I hugged him to me and tousled his hair. "Don't worry, sweetheart. We're a little upset about Junior's wife." I kissed the top of his head.

"David's mommy?"

"Yes," I said and did a double-take. Should I tell Joey about Sue Ann's death? He was bound to hear talk among the customers in the dock house.

"Why are y'all upset?" my boy asked with the innocence of youth.

"Honey, David's mommy had an accident." I hugged him close and quickly steer him away from Sue Ann. "Why don't you fill the glasses with ice while I finish getting lunch ready?" He nodded in return.

We headed back to the kitchen, where I removed the pizza from the oven and sliced it up among us. I turned the conversation toward more neutral ground, not wanting to upset Joey anymore.

Mr. Wilkes and I headed back down to the dock as the lunch crowd emptied out of Bayou Restaurant, which lay north of our marina. The DelRose family had lived and worked this dock for more than eighty years. The metal dock house, painted white with gray trim around large picture windows, housed our freezers and refrigerators for storing fish. An aluminum counter supported an antique cash register with large white numbered keys.

I walked along the dock with my back to the restaurant, jumped over a narrow breath of water, and landed on our private pier, separate from our main dock, which extended about twenty feet from the floating marina dock. The partially covered pier housed our equipment. A beautiful cedar tree shaded the pier. It smelled so good I forgot the dock house was next door. A winch attached to an overhead crane mounted to the roof of the pier held a chain that dropped into the river. The chain was hooked to a large wood crate, which rested on the bottom of the muddy Mississippi.

I pressed the button to start the generator. A loud cranking sound pierced the afternoon heat. As the crate rose out of the river, water slowly poured out the drain holes. The fish beat against the sides of the crate with a slapping sound. The winch groaned at their combined weight. I slowed the speed of the winch, allowing more water to drain off before Mr. Wilkes swung the crate onto the dock. We opened the lid. The smell of damp wood and fish feces floated up. I blew out once, and then ignored the familiar stench as thrashing fish sprayed us with their slime. I reached for a pair of clear rubber gloves and pulled them on to protect my fingers from fish scales and catfish whiskers and tied an apron over my clean jeans.

Our cleaning table was a wide aluminum sheet with three walled sides. The fourth side housed a sliding door that released unwanted creatures back into the river. The table had been built by my grandfather and allowed for easy cleaning and dressing of the fish. Mr. Wilkes awkwardly tied an apron around his lean waist. Curly gray hair molded tight to the shape of his head. His age was somewhere in the neighborhood of seventy, but he claimed he couldn't remember back that far.

I had been running this operation since coming back to Bunge County three months pregnant with Joey. I discovered I was pregnant after a very bad marriage and nasty divorce. Gran offered me a partnership if I stayed on. Gran – Lucille Diane DelRose – and Joey were my only family. I was Gran's namesake. My parents were killed in a boating accident shortly after I married. A rigging line off a tugboat fell overboard and my parents' boat motor became entangled in the ropes. The crew of the tugboat began hauling the rig out of the water, not realizing it was tangled in the motor's propeller. The smaller craft was sucked into the diesel engines, tearing it apart and killing my parents on impact. I shuddered whenever I thought about the terror they must have felt.

Mr. Wilkes flopped a dozen small catfish on the table. I grabbed the mouth of a catfish, slipped my knife from its sleeve, and then cleanly severed the head from the body. I cut away the guts, fins, and tail and pushed the bloody mess into a hole cut into the middle of the table to allow for easy cleanup. A plastic bucket hooked under the dock to catch the mess. Mr. Wilkes would motor downriver later that afternoon and dump the guts into the river.

Mr. Wilkes hefted a fifty-pound yellow catfish to a chain hoist and threaded a large steel hook inside the catfish's mouth and then out through its gills. The catfish put up one hell of a fight. His tail slapped this way and that as he tried to get free. When I was a little girl, my dad dressed-out large fish on a chain and I hated it. Now I am the fisherman and I gut fish to pay the bills.

Mr. Wilkes balanced the tip of the knife blade alongside his thumb and then slowly pierced the skin to trace an imaginary line under the catfish's gills. He continued to trace the grayish skin lengthwise, cutting ever so slightly. Laying aside the knife, he picked up needle-nose pliers and began the slow process of peeling the skin from the flesh until it lay in a folded gray heap at his feet. Sunlight shone bright on the bloody white flesh, while the catfish flung itself helplessly, gasping for breath with every jerk of the chain.

Mr. Wilkes took out another knife from his belt and effortlessly removed the flesh from the bone with one downward motion. The meat landed on the cleaning table. I took up a brush and cleaned the meat free of blood and feces and then sprayed the meat with cool water before slicing fillet strips. This process would make it easier to dredge the pieces of fish in cornmeal before dropping them into a hot kettle of oil. My customers enjoyed their fried catfish.

"Bad business that for Mr. Junior," Mr. Wilkes commented as he began filleting the other side of the yellow catfish.

"I know. I can't come to grips with it myself." I lined the fillets on a metal tray and covered them with plastic cling film.

"Some of the neighborhood boys seen Mrs. Dykes downtown leaving her car in one of them side parking lots. She was being picked up in another car." Mr. Wilkes ran cool water over the filleting knives before he slipped them back into his leather belt.

"I've heard some things, too." I grasped the handle of a metal cart laded with fish meat and pushed it toward the dock house, where we stored the fish inside a commercial refrigerator. I grabbed a canned Coke, and popped the top, and gulped the cool fizz.

"I guess the best we can do is stick by him through this mess." I pressed the cold can against my hot forehead.

"Yes, 'am, but Mr. Junior best hire him a good lawyer," Mr. Wilkes said and took a drink of Coke. He used a clean white handkerchief to wipe the sweat from his shiny face.

My thoughts exactly, I mused and then crushed the Coke can, tossing it into the garbage.

CHAPTER THREE

THE ANNUAL GRABBLING TOURNAMENT WOULD be held weekend after next at the bend in the river. The DelRose team had to be ready. Mr. Wilkes and I had teamed up for the past six years, taking on the grabbling pros throughout the area to see who could bring in the biggest catfish by hand. Last year we came close, but Junior Dykes and his partner beat us by five pounds. I had been looking forward to challenging him again. I couldn't believe Junior was involved with the killing of his wife two days ago. The sheriff was still questioning him about that night.

"I wonder who we'll be up against this year," Mr. Wilkes said.

There would be six pairs of challengers vying for the catfish trophy and a cash prize of $10,000.00 donated by various sponsors in the marine supply business. The committee chairman of the tournament had notified us this morning that Junior Dykes and his partner would not be participating this year. I'd been expecting Junior to withdraw from the tournament since we heard about Sue Ann's murder.

We put the last tray of fish into the refrigerator and sat on the picnic bench under a table umbrella. The heat was oppressive, and I had turned on the water fan, which teased us with a gentle, cool spray. Mr. Wilkes and I watched the river traffic through the waves of morning heat. A tugboat rumbled upriver, pushing six barges resting high on the water, empty of cargo. The tugboat would probably fill the barges at the Port of Vicksburg and head downriver to New Orleans. The backwash rocked us like a lullaby.

A thirty-foot cruiser, its tinted windows obscuring the occupants inside, motored past Bayou Restaurant and cut her engines when she approached our dock. My heart raced. Rene Caron jumped down from the deck of his boat and tied up at our dock. He was dressed in cut-off jeans and a white muscle shirt. His black hair was windblown and lay in a tangle about his shoulders. The sheen of sweat on his bronze skin emphasized his muscular frame. Brown eyes settled on me, and I shivered in the heat.

"Morning, Mr. Wilkes." Rene shook hands with him.

"Nice day for boating," Mr. Wilkes commented. He dug out a Coke from the ice bucket on the table in front of us and tossed it to Rene.

"Thanks," he said and sat down next to me, popping the tab. "Y'all on vacation?" he teased me, taking a big gulp of Coke. His Adam's apple moved up and down with each swallow.

"No. We worked all morning dressing fish," I said with a toss of my head. I had loosened my hair and the morning breeze blew the long strands against Rene's left arm.

He grasped the golden wheat strands between his fingers and brought them up to his lips.

I felt butterflies in the pit of my stomach. Rene was a master at seduction, but he hadn't caught me yet.

"Just stopped by to tell y'all, I'll be replacing Junior Dykes in the grabbling tournament." He gave my hair a little tug.

"What? You've never hand-grabbed fish." I sat upright and jerked my hair from his fingers.

"Little mermaid, who says I can't hand-grab? I've been going after catfish like that since I was a boy." He leaned into me.

I could feel his breath upon my face, but I didn't recoil. There was something sensual about the intimacy of the moment.

"Who'll partner you?" I blurted out, too caught up in the moment to think straight.

"My Uncle Royce," he said, and then slid along the bench closer to me under the umbrella.

I had met his uncle a few months back at the boat shop. Royce was a lot like Rene, but older. Rene was inching closer. I began to feel crowded. I almost whimpered when his skin touched mine. Mr. Wilkes had the grace to walk away from us.

"You know hand-grabbing is too dangerous for you," Rene mumbled against my cheek. His hand caressed my arm.

I felt manipulated. "What, you're afraid of a little competition?" I mocked him, and then slid away.

"No, you little fool. I just don't want to see you get hurt down there among the alligators and snakes." He took me by the shoulders and shook hard.

I jumped up from the bench and stood before him. "Rene Caron, just what do you think *I've* been doing for the past six years? Mr. Wilkes and I won the grabbling tournament two years ago," I sputtered, enraged that he would think so little of my ability.

"Yeah, and I saw just how capable you were yesterday morning when I grabbed you by the ankle and took you under," his voice dropped an octave.

"I can't believe you'd come here and insult me like this." I turned my back on him and hugged the dock railing.

"Hell, Lucy, I'm not insulting you."

I heard him walk toward me. Rene's shadow enveloped me into his private world. I melted on the spot. I could feel the heave of his chest against my back.

"You're too damned independent for your own good. Did you know that?" Rene pressed me against the railing.

I stopped breathing for a moment, wondering what he planned to do to me out here in the morning sunshine. Then Rene suddenly stepped back from me. I turned to watch him stride toward his boat, untie the rope, and jump on board.

I walked over to Mr. Wilkes.

"The man is right, Miss Lucy. You are too independent at times. Sure does get you into trouble." He chuckled and gave my hair a pull.

Men! Young or old – they all think the same way. The cruiser quickly picked up speed and entered the main channel, motoring toward the back bayou.

"Mommy?" Joey ran through dock gate. His white T-shirt showed off his tan face. He wore blue shorts and rubber dock shoes.

"Yes, honey." I wrapped my arms around his slender form, giving him a hug.

"Can we go hand-grabbing?" he asked eagerly.

"No honey. Hand-grabbing is a grown-up sport. Too dangerous for kids," I answered him. Mr. Wilkes chuckled behind me, but I ignored him. I was no kid.

"Oh, y'all have all the fun," Joey pouted.

"Hey, you can come along tomorrow when we go to the bend in the river and check out the tournament site."

"Okay, I guess," he said, giving in to me. "Mr. Wilkes, you coming, too?"

"Yes, Joey, I'll be going," Mr. Wilkes said and he strolled over to the dock house.

"Joey, get our lunch from Gran while Mr. Wilkes and I get ready for customers," I urged my son. He ran up the hill to the plantation house.

My great-grandmother had named the house *Rosebud* for the rose gardens that had been planted over the ten acres of land.

Mr. Wilkes counted the money in the antique cash register while I wiped down the aluminum tables and bench seats. I straightened the boxes made ready to pack the fish between layers of wax paper. I felt the rumble of diesel motors and looked out the picture window as two tugboats pushed their loads downriver.

The door was suddenly flung open. I jumped back. Junior Dykes stood framed in the doorway. His muscular body strained against his T-shirt and jeans. His dark brown hair fell in wavy locks across his forehead.

The look on his face was pure murder.

CHAPTER FOUR

JUNIOR SLAMMED THE DOOR SHUT and walked toward me. I was surprised to see him here.

"Them damned reporters are driving me crazy!" he thundered and sat down on the aluminum bench. He ran a hand through his hair, and then he released a heavy sigh.

"There are reporters here?" Mr. Wilkes said. He opened the door to look out.

"Not now, I ran the fools off. Their damn questions. I didn't kill Sue Ann!" His eyes were bloodshot and he sported a light brown beard.

I cleared my throat, nervous of his passionate display of temper.

"Junior, are you all right?" I said.

"Sheriff didn't have enough evidence to hold me. Forty-eight hours pacing in a ten by ten cell will drive a body crazy." Junior scratched his beard, giving it a tug now and again in a display of anger.

Mr. Wilkes sat down next to him. "Mr. Junior, you're goin' to be okay. The good Lord takes care of his own."

"Thank you, Mr. Wilkes. I appreciate it." Junior appeared to calm down a bit.

"I'm sorry, about Sue Ann." I laid a hand on his arm and squeezed. "She didn't deserve what was done to her."

Junior took my hand in his and raised it to his lips. He buried his mouth against my palm. I felt the moist touch of his tongue. Shocked, I instantly drew back. There was a time I would have wrapped my arms around him and rained his face with kisses. That was nine years ago. Junior had satisfied his raging hormones with Sue Ann. Now a half-breed Indian had a vice grip on my heart and I wasn't sure if I wanted my freedom.

"Lucy, I don't know what Sue Ann was up to these last few weeks. She'd come home late in the evening, her clothes all which-a-way. I'd try talking to her, but she'd start yelling about being trapped at home all the time, me neglecting her. I don't know." Junior stood up and began pacing. Junior was close to six foot, but the width of his body made him appear taller.

"Was she having trouble with anyone?"

"Just the late nights and bar hopping," Junior said getting choked up.

"Do you have an attorney?" I didn't want Junior to continue on his own without legal help.

"Yeah, old man by the name of Atkins." He reached for a Coke from the ice bucket we kept next to the counter for customers.

"Bruce Atkins?" Mr. Wilkes said with a look of surprise.

"Yes. Something wrong, Mr. Wilkes?" Junior moved about restlessly.

"Folks around here haven't seen Mr. Atkins in some time. He left town about five years ago to settle on the coast." Mr. Wilkes put the cash into the register and slammed it shut.

"He's still down on the coast. He's a friend of Dad's. I think the guy's okay. He got me out of jail," Junior sat down again.

"I'm glad, Junior. What happens next?" My elbows supported me as I leaned on the table toward him.

"The coroner released Sue Ann's body this morning. I have to plan her funeral. It almost killed the boys when I told them." He turned his head, but not before I saw the tears well up in his eyes.

"Junior, you should be with your sons now," I said in hushed tones.

"They're up in your house playing with Joey. The reporters keep hanging around the feed store and at the house." He banged his fist on the table.

No wonder Joey had not come down with their lunch, I thought. He was playing with the Dykes boys.

"Let's walk up hill and get lunch." I stepped around the table and took Junior's arm, encouraging him to follow. "Come on, Mr. Wilkes. We'll lock up until after lunch."

We climbed the stone steps to *Rosebud*. Junior was in a dark mood, his thoughts miles away. Children's laughter spilled from the kitchen doorway while we climbed the porch steps. Gran opened the screen door for us.

"Junior, you come on inside and let me fix you lunch," Gran said.

"Oh, Mrs. DelRose, I'm not hungry." Junior turned when his three sons ran into the kitchen with Joey at their heels.

"Daddy," young David called out. "Joey wants us to play with him some more." David was joined by his two brothers, Dennis and Daniel.

"Boys we have a full day tomorrow," Junior said, his eyes drooping from lack of sleep.

"With all the details you have to attend tomorrow, perhaps the boys would be happier if they stayed here for the night." Gran stepped in and took over. "Joey would love their company. We still have some clothes they left behind from their last visit."

"In that case – Lucy, could I speak with you on the porch?" Junior rested his hand at the base of my back. He steered me back through the screen door opening.

The boys took this as a good sign and followed Joey back to his bedroom.

The wrap-around wood porch was home to ceiling fans and comfortable outdoor furniture. Junior led me to our cushioned swing. He slid down next to me, cradling my back with his arm.

"I can trust you, Lucy. The details of the investigation were not made public. The sheriff believes the killer drove her to a deserted location and murdered her there." The Dykes family owned and operated a feed store near Rolling Fork, about fifty miles north of here. "Sue Ann left the house Saturday afternoon and no one saw her until that 911 caller discovered her body Sunday night." Junior twisted around to look at me.

"Junior, it's all so crazy. Who would want to kill her?" I could only shrug my shoulders. I hadn't been close to Sue Ann. She had been very jealous of my previous relationship with Junior. The last time I spoke with her at the grocery store a few weeks ago. She was rude and in a hurry. She was purchasing two cases of beer and had a buggy full of cocktail snacks.

"I think she began seeing someone. She'd come home smelling of liquor and marijuana. I would get so mad, but she blew me off. It's like she wanted me to kick her out. I waited for her to come home that night." Junior hung his head.

"Does the sheriff have any leads?"

"The autopsy report states the cause of death as from multiple knife wounds to the chest," Junior said with anguish.

I hugged him. He crushed me to him and I felt a shudder go through his body.

"Lucy, I need some help. The law says I killed Sue Ann because she was seeing another man. I've got to find the bastard that killed my wife." He had me by the shoulders and looked at me in earnest.

"J-Junior, you know I'll do whatever I can to help." I found myself suddenly nervous of this aggressive man.

"Thank you. I can't tell you how much this means to me and the boys." He hugged me to him again. "I want to cruise the downtown area later on this evening. I heard she use to run with a guy that frequented Blue Bird Bar & Grill."

"Yeah, but won't the sheriff have already questioned this guy?" I didn't what to stumble onto an investigation already underway.

"This isn't Bunge County we're talking about. It's Cope County law. Sheriff Umbridge has been in office since the turn of the century, and Cope County is eighty percent Umbridges. He doesn't even do investigations anymore. He assigns one of his twenty-one-year-old deputies to question possible suspects," Junior said with disgust.

"We'll look into it, Junior," I assured him. He squeezed my hand.

Lord, what had I gotten myself into?

CHAPTER FIVE

D OWNTOWN BUNGE WAS EERIE AT night. Elongated shadows
enveloped the town in mystery. The Blue Bird Bar & Grill stood
out like a peacock with its feathers fanned for all to see its artificial glory.
Cars were parked along the curb running north and south of Lincoln
Street. Neon lights glowing blue seduced Junior and me inside out of the
heat. Music spilled from its open door. The sounds of clinking glass,
relaxed laughter, and dimmed lighting wrapped us in a cocoon of
intimacy.

It felt like the most natural thing for Junior's arm to drop casually
about my shoulders while we scanned the room for an empty table. A
waitress approached us and indicated a booth at the back. A square bar
dominated the middle of the room, with chrome bar stools and tile
counters. An overhead wine rack held wine glasses hung upside down
and a wall mirror reflected the faces of the patrons as they slowly

unwound from the day's activities. Soft leather seats cushioned us as we slid into the booth decorated with the same tile-finish as the bar.

"What can I get you folks?" The waitress wore a tight nylon black mini-dress with a fitted blue vest buttoned under the roundness of her breasts. She was petite with a cloud of dark hair.

"Old Charter for me and peppermint Schnapps over ice for the lady," Junior said, tapping the table with one of the complimentary breadsticks.

I was surprised Junior remembered one of my favorite drinks after all this time.

"You see the guy at the bar." Junior indicated him with a jerk of his head. "He's one of the guys I'd seen talking with Sue Ann at the feed store." The guy was young, probably in his early twenties, light brown hair, long and straight. He reminded me of a hippie. He was talking earnestly to another guy with his back to us.

"Maybe he just wanted to know something about feed?" I suggested, not wanting to go on this witch hunt.

"No, Lucy, they talked for a long time, laughing and touching. If I didn't have a customer at the time, I would've gone over and punched him in the nose." Junior balled his hand into a fist and gave the table a whack.

Luckily the waitress came with our drinks. Junior paid her while I took a long pull on the Schnapps, tasting the sharp cool mint as it flowed over my tongue and gave me a *wow* feeling. The tight knots in my stomach began to relax. I didn't feel nervous anymore.

We knew most of this crowd. I sold fish to a lot of them during the week. Junior sold feed and garden supplies to others. Recognition dawned on them as our eyes met, but they all knew Junior and I were old friends and gave us some space. I couldn't imagine any of these people responsible for Sue Ann's death.

"Junior, I think we're on the wrong track here," I said, elbowing him in the ribs to try and divert his attention from the guy at the bar.

"How can you say that? What about him?" He jerked a thumb at the hippie again. Suddenly, the man talking to the hippie turned around on his bar stool.

Good Lord, it was Sheriff Ware of Bunge County. He was a slim man with small features. The sheriff and I had some professional history and I respected the man. Tonight he was not in uniform. Ware's bald head shone under the neon glow of advertisements along the back wall of the bar.

"Junior, let's leave it alone for now. The guy sitting next to your man is our county sheriff," I whispered to him.

Junior shook his head. "I've got to talk with this guy and see what he knew about Sue Ann."

I knew I'd lost this round. Sheriff Ware walked away toward the men's room. Without a word, Junior jumped up and walked over to the hippie. The guy didn't look happy. I could tell he recognized Junior because he drew back as Junior approached the bar.

Junior slid onto the stool vacated by the sheriff and lean toward the hippie. The exchange started out calm, but as the hippie shook his head in answer to his questions, Junior became angry.

Sheriff Ware sat down next to me on the leather bench seat.

"Miss DelRose, good to see you," he said and extended his hand.

I took it and felt his cool skin. I knew this wasn't a coincidence.

"Nice to see you again, Sheriff." I gave him a thin smile.

"Seems like you have involved yourself in another tragedy," he said with a poker face.

I was astounded he could read the situation so quickly.

"I'm not sure I understand what you mean by involvement?" I hedged.

"Junior Dykes is trying to get information from a possible witness in his wife's murder case. He is only hurting the investigation." Sheriff Ware watched the two men at the bar.

"Witness? So Junior was right in assuming this guy might know something?" I took another sip of Schnapps.

"Miss DelRose, your friend needs to let the law handle this case. Mr. Dykes has a lawyer who he can get all the information he needs through discovery of evidence," Ware reasoned.

"Yes, but there's no law that says a man can't try and protect himself," I argued.

"Is he in danger?" the sheriff countered.

"Yes, of being charged with his wife's murder."

"He has emotional ties to the victim. It's never wise to go off on a personal vendetta to find the killer. Before you know it, he accuses the wrong person and someone gets hurt." The sheriff stressed each word with a finger striking the table.

Suddenly Junior was on his feet. He had the hippie by the shirt collar. He shook the guy hard.

"Tell me, you creep," Junior said in a loud, angry voice.

Sheriff Ware jumped to his feet and signal to the bartender. Suddenly two bouncers had Junior by his arms. The sheriff said something to Junior in a hushed tone. The next thing I knew, the bouncers were escorting Junior out the front door. The sheriff patted the hippie on the back and shook his hand. The guy kept shaking his head while the sheriff talked. Finally, Sheriff Ware walked out the front door of the bar. The hippie walked over to a pay phone along the back wall.

I quickly grabbed my purse and strolled to the phone next to his. I dropped a quarter into the slot and called the number for the weather report. The hippie had the phone cradled on his shoulder and I had to strain to hear him.

"Damn straight. You said you had it under control." The hippie wasn't happy with the person at the other end of the line. "Well you tell Bubba I ain't takin' any more guff." He slammed down the receiver and stomped to the men's room.

Shit. Why did the first clue have to be a guy named *Bubba?* There must be thousands of Bubbas in the area.

Junior was standing next to his truck with Sheriff Ware, licking his pride. The two bouncers must have gone back into the bar.

"Mr. Dykes, I understand you want to get to the bottom of this, but Sheriff Umbridge did ask for my department's help in questioning witnesses in my county." Sheriff Ware leaned against Junior's Ford F-250 truck.

"I've been going nuts over this." Junior pounded his fists against the hood of his truck.

"If it were my wife, I'd be nuts too. Please go home, plan your wife's funeral. Let us work this case." The sheriff gave Junior's arm a squeeze and a reassuring pat on the back. He tipped his head to me and then headed back inside the Blue Bird Bar & Grill.

"Get in." Junior pointed to the truck. He cranked the motor and we were off. He gunned the diesel engine and took a route that headed to the riverfront landing. The river was black as ink in the night.

"What's up?" I looked at him with the help of the dash-lights. His expression was tense.

"That creep back there said something about Sue Ann meeting some guy down at the riverfront on the weekends," he mumbled through clenched teeth.

Now I understood what Sheriff Ware meant when he said Junior could hurt someone by being too close to the victim. Junior wanted revenge for what Sue Ann had put him through the past few weeks. He was looking for all the men in her life leading up to her death.

"Who was that hippie?" I said sharply.

"A wiseass who delivered farm supplies at our store. He said Sue Ann asked him for drugs, but he told her he didn't do that stuff. What a lot of horseshit. I've seen him and another driver smoking a joint back of our loading dock. I figure that's how Sue Ann got her stuff." Junior slowed down as we neared the entrance to the riverfront.

He drove between the wide brick walls to the riverfront landing, where boats could off-load into the river. Trucks were parked along the brick wall built to hold back rising flood waters. The place was deserted.

Water lapped against the concrete landing, creating white foam and tossing debris about.

Junior shifted the truck into park and then cradled his head against the steering wheel.

"Why did she do this to me? I gave her a beautiful home, wonderful kids.... I treated her good. I just don't understand." Junior's shoulders shook. He was crying.

I went numb. I had never seen Junior cry. I wrapped my arms around him and hung on.

"Don't blame yourself, Junior. Sue Ann wasn't a bad person. A little confused maybe, but that's all," I reassured him.

"Why was it so wrong being a housewife?" he cried out.

So, like a fool, I told him about *Bubba*. I had to give him hope that we had made progress in tracking down Sue Ann's killer. And that's when I put my life in jeopardy.

CHAPTER SIX

THE HUMIDITY WAS HIGH ENOUGH to wring out my shirt. Joey ran about the boat along with Junior's three sons, enjoying the excitement of being on open water as we motored to the bend in the river. Mr. Wilkes piloted the *Little Mermaid* while I kept an eye on the boys. I had promised them we would have a picnic on the sandbar after we checked out the tournament site. Our depth finder would verify the location of the barrels that had been lowered into the water last spring for this event, and the fish finder would give us an idea of the marine activity around the barrels.

"Heard you went out last night," Mr. Wilkes commented in a hushed tone. He wore his usual jean coveralls over a white T-shirt.

"Yes," I said. Now I would be in for a lecture. I knew my temper would flare when he told me to mind my own business. It was a good thing I was wearing cool white shorts with a cotton halter-top. I'd braided my hair across my shoulder, securing the end with Rene's blue ribbon.

"Mr. Junior's getting people upset with all them questions." He steered the runabout through the wake from a sight-seeing boat. "You tagging along with him makes you a target for angry folks."

Mr. Wilkes was not only our friend and employee, but our confidant. I trusted him with my life. He'd been with the DelRose family for more than forty years.

"I think he's worried he'll be charged with her murder," I lowered my voice to match his.

"I don't see how. I heard tell he was with Miss Leah Ellis last weekend on a business trip." Mr. Wilkes turned to face me.

"Junior said he was home with the boys waiting for her to come back." The wind tore my words from my lips as Mr. Wilkes thrust the throttle to maximum speed. The boys squealed with delight and hung on for dear life.

"Miss Lucy, I'd tell you to stay out of this, but knowing you, I guess I'm too late." He glared at me.

I turned my back on him and gazed at the passing landscape. The Mississippi bank was flushed with grass and vegetation. From time to time, catfish jumped from the water and flicked their tails at us. Louisiana's sloping banks were peppered with magnolia blossoms and crepe myrtles.

I thought about what Mr. Wilkes had said. Leah Ellis was the bookkeeper at the Dykes feed store. I had seen her couple of times in the past. I knew she was single. She was also young and very pretty. Suddenly I felt a little sorry for Sue Ann.

Mr. Wilkes idle the motor and we coasted in at the bend in the river. It was about a mile past Turtle Island. He turned on the depth finder and we checked the water depth – six feet. The shape of the six round barrels showed up on our sonar. The boys crowded around to see for themselves. The fish finder honed in on fish in the area, picking up several sizes, one or two large enough for hand-grabbing. I showed Joey how to distinguish the different species of fish. Junior's boys were very quick to pick up on how the digital instruments worked.

"Let's find a good spot for our picnic." I tapped Mr. Wilkes on the arm. I wanted to keep Junior's boys from dwelling on their mother's death.

"Okay boys, hold on." He whipped the wheel toward Louisiana and increased the throttle until we broke into the main channel. The *Little Mermaid* flew over rough current to the shadow depths near an enormous sandbar north of Turtle Island. There was shade from the crepe myrtle trees and clean sand where we could spread the blanket for our picnic.

Twin diesel engines rumbled downriver. A thirty-foot cruiser broke through the backwash of a tugboat laden with barges that was heading toward New Orleans. I grabbed a pair of binoculars from the boat and trained the glasses on the cruiser. A black-haired beauty wearing nothing but a band-aid across her crotch and two dots to cover her breasts was stretched out on a beach blanket at the stern of the boat – sunbathing. It felt like someone punched me in the gut. Rene exited the pilothouse wearing swimming trunks over his narrow hips. My heart did a flip-flop. I recognized Jetta, a gypsy woman I'd once knocked flat on her ass with a right-hand punch. She was a barefoot nightmare with a fowl mouth and a habit of showing up when I least expected it. Up to now, Rene had assured me Jetta was history. I swallowed a painful lump in my throat. Sue Ann and I became one.

I lowered the binoculars and watched the cruiser until she was out of sight. The men in my life always seemed to want women who gave their favors freely. I lost Junior in college because I won't give in to sex before marriage. Now it looked like I'd lost Rene because I feared commitment after my abusive marriage. I twisted the blue ribbon from my braid and tossed it into the Mississippi River.

The trip home was quiet. The boys were exhausted from swimming in the intense heat. Tomorrow would be a painful day for them. They would say a final good-bye to their mother. Gran and I planned to attend the service while Joey stayed with Mr. Wilkes at the marina.

Mr. Mack, Junior's dad, was on the dock with Gran when we eased into the boat slip. Mr. Wilkes pressed the button to raise the boat out of the water, and I roused the drowsy boys.

"Grandpa," David cried out. He jumped from the boat and ran to Mr. Mack. The old man crouched down on one knee to wrap his arms around his grandsons as they threw themselves on him one by one. Mr. Mack blinked his eyes several times. I knew he was holding back the tears. The boys meant everything to him.

CHAPTER SEVEN

SUE ANN WAS LAID OUT like a queen. The mortician did a wonderful job of creating a vision in white. The Dykes family occupied the first two pews. Gran and I sat behind Mr. Mack and Junior. The priest consoled the boys as they stood next to the pew. The funeral started with song and prayer. Incense burned alongside the coffin while I put a handkerchief against my nose. I hate the smell.

By the end of the service, Junior's boys were crying. Through their tears, they were escorted down the aisle toward the back of the church, along with their father and grandpa. Gran and I followed at a distance. The coffin was wheeled out of the church. Six pallbearers grasped the brass handrails and carried it to the hearse. When the driver slammed the door of the hearse shut, I flinched.

Sue Ann's final drive through Bunge County would take place on a hot, cloudless day. I took Gran by the elbow and steered her toward our station wagon. The Dykes family had many friends, so the funeral procession took a while. Once we finally reached the cemetery, Gran and I walked to the tent covering the open grave. More than twenty white funeral chairs were lined up next to the gravesite. Junior indicated for Gran and me to sit with the family, and I smiled my gratitude. Gran wasn't up to standing for long periods of time. Mr. Mack kept his grandsons close to him. The priest read over Sue Ann, and then each of her sons placed a flower upon the coffin. Last of all, Junior took a rose from his lapel and placed it next to the boys' flowers. The crowd began to break up. The priest hovered over Junior and the boys one last time before the gravedigger's shovel tossed the dirt upon the coffin with a harsh thud. I wanted to cover my ears. No one should go out like that — not a mother of three small boys.

Gran was tiring. I helped her into the station wagon and walked around to the driver's side. Junior left his family and came over to me.

"I'm going out tonight after the boys are asleep. I need to track down this Bubba character." Junior looked tired. His eyes were bloodshot and droopy. He already had a five o'clock shadow.

"Junior, please go home and stay there. Don't leave the boys tonight." I squeezed his forearm.

"Maybe you're right," he said. He ran a hand through his ruffled hair, then leaned toward me and kissed my cheek.

I patted his shoulder and gave him a weak smile. Leah Ellis' face swam before my eyes. I hoped Junior was not a womanizer like my ex-husband or — Rene.

"Get some sleep. Have your dad bring the boys over as soon as you can," I urged.

He nodded and then bent down to speak with Gran through the opened door.

"Mrs. DelRose, I appreciate your coming." Junior's boyish charm shone through his misery.

"Nonsense, Junior, we're like family."

"I feel the same way." His face relaxed. David ran to his father and buried his face against Junior's slacks. Junior cupped the boy's head.

I watched the Dykes family climb into the black limo and drive off.

"I feel so bad for those boys," Gran said and wiped a tear from her cheek.

I patted her hand.

"I can't imagine Joey going through something like that." Gran wiped another tear.

"He won't," I assured her.

"What, with you taking all kinds of chances . . ." Gran blew her nose into a tissue.

"Gran, I can't promise you that I won't get hurt a time or two, but I'll take no more chances than you have over the years." I gave her an impish grin.

"They were right, you're just like me," she said with pride.

Thank God, I thought and headed toward home.

I drove along the scenic route, knowing Gran would enjoy the river view. Tree limbs swayed as the wind tossed them like sticks. I felt the wind's pull on the steering wheel and noticed dark clouds moving in from the west. A summer storm was brewing. The river seemed to take on a menacing purpose, tossing small craft about like play toys. I slowed my speed, taking the next curve with caution. A shadow in my peripheral view had me taking a second glance in my rearview mirror. A dark blue truck was too close for comfort, I increased my speed a tad, but so did the truck's driver. A right turn was up ahead and I flicked on the turn signal so this idiot would get off my ass.

Then I felt a jolt. I glanced in the rearview mirror. The assault on my bumper wasn't an accident. The truck bore down upon us again.

"Gran, hold tight," I yelled, and then slammed on my brakes.

The screeching sound of rubber against pavement resonated as our bumpers crashed. The truck shoved the station wagon toward the protective railing. Somewhere in my mind, I heard Gran scream. I fought our attacker, wrenching the steering wheel left with all my strength to keep us from the turbulent waters below. The truck didn't let up. The monster spun its wheels, eating rubber as it crumbled the bumper, forcing our station wagon against the railing. The metal rail snapped under the weight of two vehicles. Gran screamed again. Our station wagon hung like a sick puppy over the edge of the cliff before one final shove sent us over. I drowned out Gran's scream with my own as the river rushed up to meet us.

CHAPTER EIGHT

WE CRASHED INTO THE RIVER headfirst and bobbed like a cork. My neck whipped forward, striking the windshield. An explosion of stars blinded me. Gran was secured by her seatbelt, but I'd seen her head snap forward, too, and then bounce off the neck support of her seat. We swayed there a few seconds before the car sank into a watery grave. The cold water shocked me into action. I tore at the clasp of my seatbelt and then frantically wrenched Gran free of hers. I scrambled over the front seat, dragging Gran with me. The second set of seats was easier to flip over. We crawled to the rear of the station wagon. Gran hugged against me as I bent down to release the emergency button that automatically opened the wagon's rear door. Terror gripped me when the seal of our coffin broke and all hell began pouring in.

"Hold your breath," I screamed. Then the swift current slammed against us. I held fast to the handrail along the wall of the wagon and shoved Gran through the opening, fighting the rush of silt and debris bouncing off us. Once freed from the vehicle, I balanced momentarily against the tailgate and then pushed off to the surface. Air bubbles escaped my lips. I was running out of air. *Please, God, please get Gran to the surface*. I grasped her rear-end and heaved. *Please. Please*. I kicked and wiggled my way toward the surface as the strong current took the breath from my body. Gran was swimming. God bless her! Her long gray hair floated about us in a cloud of hope. Then Gran broke free of the river. I couldn't make it. Darkness descended.

Hands fumbled about me. I tried opening my eyes, but they were bleary from silt. Male voices shouted as I was placed on my back. Lips covered mine. I felt the pressure of air entering my lungs. I struggled to breathe on my own. Lips released mine. I turned on my side and threw up muddy river water. When I fell back, I noticed thunder clouds darkening the sky. Rain began drumming against my head. I tried to see Gran, but there were too many bodies around. I sensed we were on a crew boat with many workers onboard. Hours seem to pass in my muddled state. At one point, I was being carried by strong arms. I felt helpless as a kitten.

"Lucy," Gran's strong voice broke through the mélange.

"Gran," I mumbled, by voice hoarse. Someone cleaned me up with wet towels and then I was wrapped in a warm, thick blanket. My forehead hurt where the windshield had struck it. Sunburned men in jeans and muscle shirts moved us indoors. Rain pelted the pilothouse. Gran's blanket quivered from her shaking body, and I could see a lump forming on her forehead. A short while later, the crew gave us hot tea with lemon. The more I drank, the better I felt. I was so worried about Gran, but she was busy drilling the captain about an instrument gauge he was using to check the barometer.

"I should've known it would rain today," Gran said. "The barometer shows the humidity at one hundred and two percent." Gran drank her tea, being her normal, calm self.

My eyes had finally cleared and I began to feel safe inside my blanket. I looked out the windows of the small tugboat and noticed that the boat was not burdened by a load. That meant the crew was probably headed upriver to the Port of Vicksburg.

The captain entered the pilothouse and came over to Gran and me. He was an elderly man, gray at the temples, about average height with a broad grin. The crew referred to him as Captain John.

"I'm happy to see the two of you doing better," Captain John said.

"I want to thank you for fishing us out," I said. I liked this capable man, so at home behind the wheel.

"We saw the car go off the cliff and hit the water," said a member of the crew. "To tell you the truth, we didn't think you'd make it," He stepped forward from the rest.

He was a rough looking character with braided hair and earring studs. Something told me he was the one who'd given me mouth to mouth resuscitation. He reached out a hand and took mine.

"I'm glad you came around, miss," he said in broken English and I could tell he was more comfortable using his native language, Spanish.

"Thank you," I spoke softly, giving him a grateful smile. My hair, like Gran's, had dried in a cloud about my shoulders. Wet clothes clung to my skin, leaving nothing to the imagination. Thank goodness for the blankets.

"Ladies, it's none of our business, but why'd that truck shove you off the cliff?" Captain John said.

"I don't know. We'd just come from a funeral on our way home." I waved my hand to emphasizing my frustration. But Sue Ann's killer had just given me a second clue.

"I radioed the sheriff's department. They'll meet us dockside at the grain elevator." Captain John laid a reassuring hand upon my shoulder and squeezed.

"I don't know what we would have done if you and your crew hadn't been here," Gran said in her matron's tone.

"Ma'am, it was an honor." With that said, the crew went back to work readying the tugboat for docking.

Sheriff Ware was dockside. We were assisted down the ramp, the rain easing up.

"Sheriff, I turn the ladies over to you," Captain John said with ceremony.

"Thank you, Captain." The sheriff shook hands with him.

The deputies loaded us into the sheriff's car. I watched two deputies questioning the crew.

The Blue Bird Bar & Grill had come back to haunt me. I shivered next to Gran.

Which Bubba had tried to kill us?

CHAPTER NINE

S HERIFF WARE LET ME KNOW in no uncertain terms to lay off the Sue Ann Dykes case if I didn't want another dip in the Mississippi River.

I wasn't eager to pursue the issue myself, but the last few weeks of Sue Ann's life bothered me. She was a young woman who had married into a wealthy family, had three beautiful boys, and then suddenly began running around with other men. Had Junior gave her a good reason? The image of Leah Ellis swam before me. The cool beauty of the woman's face would entice Junior if he felt saddled with a nagging wife. I could still hear his anguished words last night while we parked riverside. Did Junior make Sue Ann feel unattractive? Was he now guilt-ridden for an indiscretion with Leah? I moan into my hands at the disturbing conclusions that swam in my head.

Joey danced about Gran and I while we cleaned up after our ordeal in the river. He listened to the story four times between us. Mr. Wilkes came up to the house and sat at the kitchen table. He listened to Joey tell our story for the fifth time.

"Miss Lucille, I don't like it, not one bit," he said, cracking the knuckles of his long thin fingers.

"Oh, Mr. Wilkes, I think it's so cool," Joey said. "Can I tell my friends?" He ran to the phone, looking back over his shoulder.

"Joey, I think we need to recover a bit before you go telling the story again," Gran said gently. She took Joey by the shoulders and pointed him toward the kitchen sink. "How about filling the dishwasher for me?"

"Sure, Gran." Joey gave her a look of hero worship.

The doorbell rang. When I opened the front door, there stood news anchor woman Rachel Becker and her cameraman.

"Rachel!" I knew why she was here. News travels fast in Bunge County.

"Mind if we come in?" she said and eased her way past me. At five foot ten inches, there wasn't much point in arguing with her. Rachel's cameraman was like a puppy being led on a leash.

I escorted her to the library, but Gran had already gotten a look at our visitors as we rounded the corner into the hallway. Gran shook her head. I felt the same way. I followed the newspeople into the library and closed the door.

"The news waves are buzzing about you and your grandmother. What's going on?" Rachel eased down on the sofa. An amazing feat, considering the pencil-thin skirt she wore. Rachel was all business.

"Rachel, you know as much as I do. Gran and I were coming home from Sue Ann Dykes' funeral when this blue truck started ramming us from behind. I tried to avoid it, but this character was determined to send us over the hill." I shuddered, still struggling to free myself of that claustrophobic underwater nightmare.

"Lucy, are you helping Junior track down Sue Ann's killer?" Rachel looked excited, as if the idea was bubbling with possibilities.

"No, Rachel, I'm just helping a friend get through a difficult time," I said playing down Junior's manhunt.

"Lucy, this is Rachel you're talking to. Level with me." She took my hand and pulled me down next to her on the sofa. Her cameraman wandered innocently around the library while Rachel reeled me in.

"Look, Rachel, some creep pushed me and Gran into the river. I don't know why. I hope the sheriff can find out. To try and hurt me is one thing, but Gran is ninety-one years old." I allowed Rachel to drape an arm around my shoulders.

"I'm sorry, my dear. You know I have a job to do."

She smelled of Chanel No. 5 and her dark hair was swept up in a French twist. Rachel was an old college friend. She'd hunted deer with me over the years. We were pals.

"Look, just say it was an accident until Sheriff Ware proves otherwise." I edged closer to the end of the sofa and stood up.

"Lucy, I'll play it down, but I wish you'd let me know if anything else happens. My hunch is that Junior's got you messed up in Sue Ann's murder."

Rachel was not far off the mark.

She got up and made for the door, with her cameraman trailing behind. I showed them out and went back into the kitchen.

"That newswoman wanted a story, didn't she?" Gran said.

"Afraid so," I said. My nerves were still humming. My terror over Gran's near-miss wouldn't subside. Who wanted us dead?

"I put a call into our insurance company. They'll cover the car loss. Maybe we should go out tomorrow and look at new station wagons." Gran continued muttering to herself as she moved about the kitchen.

I worried that Gran was in some sort of denial about the seriousness of the accident.

Suddenly the telephone rang, causing us all to jump.

"Hello," I answered.

"Meet me down at the dock," Rene Caron said in a commanding voice.

I wanted to tell him to take a flying leap, but after the day I'd had, I couldn't. "Sure," I mumbled.

"Lucy, dear, who was that?" Gran turned from the sink, where she was giving Joey a hand with the dishes. The bump on her forehead was more pronounced than it had been earlier, but she seemed to be okay.

"Rene wants to talk to me. I'll be down at the dock." I made a hasty exit, trying to ignore the knowing look on Mr. Wilkes' face.

I skipped down the hill toward the river with my hair flying out behind me. The day was at half-mask. The dock bell rang a greeting while I took in Rene's bronze good looks. His black hair stirred about his shoulders and I could see his chest muscles flex as he moved toward me. His shadow blocked out the afternoon sun as he loomed over me. I expected a shouting match, but his large hands grasped my waist and he lifted me up against his chest. I felt the quiver of his body as his arms tightened about me. A lump formed in my throat and I could not speak. Jetta's naked body laid claim to the edge of my conscious, but my near-death experience won out. I needed to feel his arms around me.

Rene's skin smelled of cedar. I dug my fingers into his black mane and hugged his neck. Suddenly, the cold river grave came back to haunt me and I tasted my own tears as I cried softly against his neck. He patted me like a kitten and murmured my name over and over. I couldn't believe this dangerous creature could be so tender, so caring of my safety. Rene felt warm and his muscles were firm under my fingers. I caressed his face and traced the hawk-like nose, lingering on full, kissable lips. My mouth found his and I drew him into me, bringing my body tighter against him until the roundness of my breasts flattened against his chest. My nipples hardened, and I couldn't get enough of him. He lifted me into his arms and carried me inside the dock house and pressed my back against the wall. His thighs were so strong and giving. His lips left mine and his tongue traced my neck and settle against the hollow of my throat. I purred like a kitten.

"I nearly lost you, Lucy," he mumbled against my breast. His mouth slipped beneath my bra, searching for my nipple. He tugged and pulled on the hardening mound until I cried out and pressed his face tighter to my breast.

"I want you in my bed." His voice dropped an octave.

Oh, boy!

My knees began to tremble. I hung onto him. My head fell back against his shoulder, allowing him complete access to my neck. I liked the tickle sensation of his mouth and tongue when they left my breast and moved upward. He nibbled my ear, then took the lobe into his mouth and sucked gently. I nearly swooned. His knee separated my legs. I found myself astride his muscular thigh; my shorts rode high over my soft butt cheeks. I groaned when his fingers slipped inside my shorts then under my panties. He was fast discovering my secrets. Shivers sprinkled down upon me.

Then the image of Jetta sprawled on his boat half-naked hit me between the eyes. He couldn't possibly want to make love to me after having an afternoon with that gypsy woman, could he? Sue Ann and her life with Junior put me in doubt. I pushed back from Rene and reluctantly slid off his leg. It took Rene a couple of heartbeats before he realized I no longer wanted him.

He reached out for me, but I sidestepped him.

He looked confused and then wounded. Maybe I was wrong about Jetta.

"Lucy, come home with me," he said, caressing the wheat strands, which still clung to his arms.

"How many women do you usually bed in a week?" The words tumbled out, but I couldn't stop them. I was jealous of Jetta. The thought of him touching her was too much for me.

"What do you mean?" He stepped back from me.

"Jetta is what I'm talking about. I saw the two of you on the river yesterday. For God's sake, Rene, she was practically naked." My voice rose as I stood hands on hips, staring up at him.

"I saw you and the boys on the sandbar. Had it occurred to you that she may have stowed away?" Rene's voice raised a couple of notches, too.

"How does one stow away on a cabin cruiser?" I couldn't see sense. All I saw was Jetta's naked body and Rene in an attractive swimsuit.

"Lucy, you have my word. Jetta snuck on board when I was at the riverfront loading supplies. She hid under the stern rigging. When I came out of the pilothouse, she was in a bikini. I threw her off the boat near shore, a few hundred yards downriver."

He reached for me, pressing his body against mine; his hand cupped my chin before his lips roughly covered my lips. His tongue probed my inner soul. But I just couldn't believe he was telling the truth. My past experience with my ex-husband made me see red. I pushed him away from me.

"Rene, I don't trust men in general." I wanted him to understand my feelings.

"So I'm to believe that you and Junior going bar hopping was okay?" His harsh words floored me.

"I know it looked that way, but it wasn't," I said, defending myself.

"Exactly how I feel," Rene said. He ran his fingers through my hair and then yanked me back to him.

The bell rang above the door, dragging me down to earth.

"Oh, dear me," the Mayor's wife said. She brought her hand to her mouth. "You're open for business, aren't you?"

Rene released me.

"Yes, ma'am, we are," I said.

Mr. Wilkes came through the door.

"I'll pick you up tonight for dinner," Rene said, and then gave me a little pat on my bottom.

What crust!

CHAPTER TEN

MY POLISHED COTTON DRESS MADE a swishing sound as it rubbed against my nylon hose. I descended the stone steps to the marina dock. Rene said he'd be here around eight o'clock. Why I wanted to see him after his lame excuse about Jetta, I don't know. My heart wanted to believe, but past experience with my ex-husband gnawed at me.

The sun struck a deal with the sky for one last splash of color, then it slipped under a blanket of night. The crickets sang their sweet song. I held a wisp of scarf in my right hand, ready to cover my long hair against the wind while cruising in Rene's thirty-footer.

The roar of twin engines approached the dock, and I steadied my heart with a hand on my chest, ready for Rene's dark good looks. The lanterns picked up the shadows of a cabin cruiser sliding in on its own backwash. It wasn't Rene. I turned to head back uphill.

"Lucy, hang on," came the urgent voice of Junior Dykes. His dark, curly hair was a tangle about his shoulders. There was a wild look in his eyes. "Come on, Lucy, I found the hideout." He jumped onto the dock and grabbed my arm.

"Junior, what in the hell's going on?" I tried to wrestle free from his grasp.

Junior turned back towards the water, still gripping my arm. "Come on, I found where Sue Ann's been seeing this guy," he said over his shoulder and manhandled me onto his boat. The small cabin cruiser was lit within.

I grabbed the handrails along the console, ready to jump back onto the dock. Junior had other ideas. He gunned the motor and sent the dock rocking furiously in our wake.

"Junior, what's the meaning of this? You can't just kidnap me." I franticly tied the scarf about my hair. I knew that Junior wasn't really kidnapping me. I was just damn mad at him for interrupting my evening. Rachel's words came back to haunt me.

"Kidnapping? I thought you wanted to help me find Sue Ann's killer?" He gave me a look of dismay.

"Yes, of course I do, Junior, but not like this." I laid a hand upon his arm. He was steering the cruiser north. "I had plans tonight."

Junior seemed to notice my dress and heels for the first time.

"I'm sorry, Lucy. I get kind of crazy sometimes." He ran a hand through his hair, but his speed stayed constant. "I can't lose this lead."

I sighed and walked away from Junior, then stepped down into the cabin. I called Gran on my cell phone to let her know what was happening.

"Lucy, I don't like this one bit. Tell Junior to bring you right back," she ordered me.

"Gran, he's like a man on a mission."

"I don't care. Someone's going to get hurt… Oh dear," she said. There was silence for a couple of seconds.

"Lucy, where's Dykes taking you?" Rene sounded angry and worried at the same time.

"We're heading north in his small cabin cruiser." My heart raced at hearing Rene on the other end of the phone. "He's in some kind of state about his wife's killer. Said something about getting a lead on where Sue Ann met with a man."

"I'm on my way. Call me before you dock. Don't get out of that boat, whatever you do," Rene commanded and then he was gone.

"Lucy, stay close to the boat," Gran urged.

"Okay, Gran. Don't let Joey know what's happening."

"I won't, honey. He's playing his Wii game."

We said good-bye. I peeked out the pothole and saw Louisiana rushing up to meet us. We were about six miles north of the Mississippi River bridges. On a barge secured to a stake driven deep into a sandbar, there was a party in progress. Country and western music bubbled all around the cruiser. I stepped onto the deck and caught sight of Junior sliding a .22 caliber automatic pistol at his back down the waistband of his jeans. Now, I was really anxious. I tapped out Rene's cell number.

"Lucy, I see the cruiser up ahead. For God's sake, don't let Junior crash the party. It's being given by one of my clients for his employees." Rene sounded frustrated beyond reason.

"To hell with the party!" I yelled into the phone. Junior bumped into me and knocked the phone out of my hands. It skidded across the deck and into a live well full of water.

Junior dropped anchor and jumped overboard. A big splash had river water cascading about me.

"Hurry up, Lucy. I'll catch you," Junior urged me from below.

I looked down. Black ink lapped about Junior's knees. "No thank you. My dress isn't drip-dry. I'll wait for you here." I waved him away.

"No, dammit. Lucy, jump," Junior screamed up at me, his face a shadow of fury.

The party made so much noise no one overheard our conversation. Lanterns swayed in time with the music. The band struck up another song, and the revelers danced to the tune. I looked down at Junior and knew he was not in his right mind. How could I keep him from crashing the party and hurting people?

Rene's thirty-footer eased in next to us and I heaved a sigh of relief. Then Junior hoisted himself over the rail of the cruiser. He gathered me up in his arms and threw me into the river. I screamed with indignation. What the hell! Another wet, ruined evening in my life of abstinence.

Junior dropped down next to me. Next thing I knew, he'd hauled me out of the river and onto the sandbar. My pantyhose fell about my knees and I lost my high-heels in the wet sand. Junior had me by the wrist and he was not letting up.

Rene appeared at my side, wet and scary-looking. He clipped Junior at the knee, and Junior went down on the grainy sand, taking me with him. Rene grabbed Junior by his shirt collar and hauled him back into the water. Junior's hand loosened about my wrist and I wrestled free, then stepped back onto the sandbar and leaned down to pull off my wet pantyhose and my damp scarf. I tried to find my shoes while the guys wrestled about in the river.

The revelers continued to party. Nothing could interrupt their alcohol high. At last, Rene gave Junior a final blow to the chin. Junior sank in the water and Rene dragged his dead weight back onto the sand.

"He's got a gun in his waistband." I indicated with a finger, then flopped down on the sand, disgusted at my appearance. Rene still managed to look great in wet jeans and tank top. He retrieved the weapon.

"What's going on here, Lucy?" Rene dropped down next to me.

"I don't know. One minute I'm waiting for you, and the next Junior throws me on his boat and off we go." Junior had never been this unpredictable before.

"Let me get a friend on the barge to run Junior back across the river," Rene said. He took off toward the barge, which was staked at the other end of the sandbar, and walked across a catwalk to the party.

Poor Junior, I thought as I combed his hair from his eyes. He looked so peaceful. Maybe the only peace he's had since the murder. Then

Junior began to stir. His eyes popped open and looked back and forth like a horse about to bolt.

"Junior, its Lucy. You're okay. Rene's going to get one of the guys to pilot you back to Bunge." I laid a hand upon his shoulder.

Junior shook me off and jumped to his feet. "We're almost there, Lucy." He pointed to an opening in the woods. "There's a camp down the road. That's where she met him." He pulled me to my feet and wrapped his right arm around my shoulders.

"Junior, please. I can't take much more." I fought his arm, but he was having done of it.

He dragged me to the wood's edge. I screamed out Rene's name, but the music swallowed the sound.

"Come on, darling. I need you to help me." Junior pulled me close to him.

I smelled the river mud clinging to his shirt and shivered at his determination. I wanted to get this over with tonight. Whatever had him so crazy, we might as well get to the root of it?

"Let's hurry, Junior." I pulled at him until he finally let me run toward the dirt road in bare feet. Sticks and rocks jabbed my tender arches. Junior broke into a run to keep up with me. An abandoned campsite appeared through the trees. When I saw the condition of the camp, I knew Sue Ann would never come here. The place was falling apart.

"Where is he, Junior?" I danced around the campsite. "Over here behind the fire-pit? Maybe he's hiding in that rotten hut over there?" I pointed to a building with no roof and broken windows.

Junior stood still. Water dripped from his hair and down his cheeks. He looked like he was crying. He rubbed his eyes with the palms of his hands. Light from the moon shone upon him, a forlorn figure in a melodrama.

Like a woman, I folded. I stepped up to him, cupped his face within my palms and kissed him gently upon the lips to calm him down. His manner changed and he gently pulled me to him, rocking me gently.

"I'm sorry, Lucy." My friend was back.

Rene came thundering through the woods with some of the revelers in time to see us embrace. I gestured to Rene to hold off.

"How about we go back to Bunge?" I eased an arm around Junior's waist and urged him back toward the river. He was still brooding a little, but allowed me to pull him along. When I came level with Rene, I stopped and stepped away from Junior.

"Sorry, Caron," Junior said. "I didn't mean to scare Lucy. I'm going home." He gave Rene a friendly whack on the back and walked on ahead of the revelers.

"Rene, I'm worried. Maybe we should call his father to meet us at the riverfront?" I laid my hand on Rene's arm, but he shook it off. I looked into his eyes and knew he didn't like Junior kissing me. "It wasn't anything but a friendly kiss to calm him down." I held Rene's glaze until he slipped an arm around my waist. My hair became caught on his watchband. He removed the watch and pocketed the timepiece. The revelers jostled one another as they followed us.

Junior was already onboard his cruiser. We heard the motor crank. Before we could stop him, Junior backed into Rene's thirty-footer. Rene released me abruptly and dived into the river, surfacing to climb a ladder onto his boat deck. His cruiser was made of thick gauge aluminum. No bump from a smaller vessel could damage it. The revelers and I watched in bemused horror while the two men tried to outflank the other. Junior's apologetic manner had been a ruse. He was out to get even with Rene for knocking him out.

An older gentleman came up to me and held out his hand. He was a slender man dressed in western clothes. "Hello, my name's Buck Sanders. I'm the one giving this party." We shook.

"Sorry about the intrusion," I said, unable to take my eyes off the cruisers.

Then the sheriff's patrol boat whipped across the channel, lights flashing as she came about between the cruisers. Someone had decided to call the law.

CHAPTER ELEVEN

I PEELED OFF MY DRESS and panties and tossed them into a small hamper in a bathroom on Rene's cruiser. Rene had given me a terry cloth robe to wear until we got back to Bunge. Suddenly I realized that I hadn't heard the outboard motors humming. I peered out the porthole. We were anchored upriver. Junior had been escorted back to Bunge by deputies. Rene was still steaming over the minor damage Junior had caused his cruiser. Men and their egos!

My hair was a mess. I tried to comb out the river mud, but to no avail. Damned Junior Dykes for ruining my evening — just because I had felt sorry for him. I was beginning to think Junior was suffering more from guilt than loss of his wife. The doorknob rattled.

"Lucy, come here." Rene opened the bathroom door. He had a towel wrapped loosely about his waist. "Let's go take a shower back in the stern compartment."

Oh, boy, I thought, watching the way his towel draped his hips.

"Jetta," I mumbled. He looked delicious in that skimpy towel.

"Who?" His eyes bore into mine.

My stomach fell about my ankles as I followed him past a large bunk made up with deep blue sheets and matching comforter. The bath was equipped with a shower enclosed in frosty thick glass. I dropped my terry robe to the floor, wanting — no — needing him to see me. Rene's eyes burned a trail over my body. His towel joined mine. I gasped. I had never seen a male body so perfect in every way.

This was crazy, just crazy, but I stayed rooted to the spot.

Rene adjusted the flow of water that poured through the jet streams and we stepped inside the stall. He turned me under the flow of the jets and I closed my eyes to enjoy the warmth of the water. He shampooed my hair, running his fingers through the long strands. I lay my head upon his chest while he rubbed conditioner through it.

"Open your eyes, little mermaid," he commanded.

I did better than that. I stood on my tiptoes and encircled his neck with my arms. I felt his muscles tense when I slid my wet body over him, touching his erection with my inner thighs. I wrapped my legs around his waist, letting him carry my weight. I brushed my lips against his throat, feeling the heat of his flesh and tasting the moistness of his skin. My fingers traveled down his arm to the soap dish. I pick up the bar of soap and washed his shoulders, chest, and back while I teased his nipples with mine. I rubbed the soap over me creating a slick, foamy lather between us. I shampooed his hair, feeling the thickness of the strands and the shape of his skull. He groaned. He turned around and water cascaded over us while the soap trickled down the drain, leaving our bodies squeaky clean. He pulled my head back and I tasted the thrust of his tongue and wrapped myself more into him now that we were one.

The misty steam created a haven for our bodies when we moved together in mutual fulfillment. The water mirrored the lights, and I saw his proud face and hawk-like nose looking down at me in wonder and pride.

Suddenly the boat was ramped from the rear. We fell against the shower door.

"What the hell?" Rene said, stepped out of the shower, grabbed a towel, and wrapped it around his waist as he bolted upstairs on deck.

I followed with a towel around my wet body.

Junior's laughter carried back to us from across the river. "Fuck you, Caron."

"Damned you to hell, Dykes!" Rene said and spotlighted him in the night.

Junior's boat hit a wave of backwash from a passing tugboat that nearly swamped him.

Rene switched off the light. "He's loose cannon, alright." He slipped an arm around me and drew me to him. His lips were warm.

"Rene, you take my breath away," I said with a sigh. This bizarre night was still upon me.

"I want you and Joey to live with me." He brushed his lips across my throat. "I don't want to let you out of my sight."

Passionate heat warmed my blood, I wanted him so. He hadn't mentioned marriage, and being a mother of a small boy, I could never move in with a man without a permanent commitment. Rene's apartment was built within his massive welding shop. A luxury apartment equipped with an aquarium big enough to swim in — to the delight of Joey.

Junior's boat disappeared into the black bayou.

"Rene, I can't leave Rosebud Plantation without more of a commitment from you." There I said it. I waited for his withdrawal, but it did not come.

"I'm still carrying a lot of baggage that I need to get rid of." His fingers moved across my belly. "I want to be able to give you and Joey all that I have."

I felt my stomach muscles tighten at his honesty, yet the ambiguity of his *baggage* made me nervous. Did I want to walk away from this man? I couldn't live with him now, but I still wanted him.

We finally dressed. Rene helped me with my damp panties, bra, and dress — all the while caressing, kissing, and playing with me until I went nuts. I helped him with his briefs, jeans, and T-shirt, my tongue playing with him throughout, until he backed me up against the wall and branded me with a kiss so tender I wanted to cry.

"I'm letting you off the hook for now, little mermaid," he murmured against my lips. "You belong to me — you and Joey – so don't go making any other plans." I felt the strength in his arms as he lifted me up to plant a kiss on my nose.

"Yes, sir," I saluted him with my right hand.

"Fresh." He dropped me back on my feet, but gave my bottom a sharp slap.

"Hey," I complained, rubbing my backside.

It was way after midnight before Rene brought me home. He walked me up to the porch and into the kitchen. Everyone was asleep.

"I don't want to go." Rene wrapped his arms around me, brushing sweet kisses across my face.

I playfully rubbed myself against him, letting my hands slip in and out of his damp jean pockets, teasing him to life. Suddenly something hit the brick floor and made a clattering noise. I looked down and saw Rene's watch reflecting the kitchen lights. I laughed at my clumsiness and stooped to pick it up. I started to hand it back to Rene, but something caught my eye — words engraved on the backside of the watch.

To Rene with love, Jetta.

CHAPTER TWELVE

WITH THE SMELL OF HIM still clinging to my skin, I turned my back. I knew I shouldn't be jealous of Jetta. She came before me, but dammit, did he have to wear her watch on a date with me?

Rene took the watch and flipped it over. He swore out loud. He threw the watch onto the brick floor and stomped it with his heel until he flatten the metal.

"Jetta did not give me that watch. I bought it years ago off a guy on an oil rig." He pulled me back against him, rubbing his hands up and down my arms, flattening the cotton dress against my flesh. "I can't explain how Jetta got the watch engraved. We were close in the past, but not anymore. She must have swiped it back then." His lips and tongue began working their magic.

"Rene, it's none of my business…" I tried to sound nonchalant, but I couldn't pull it off. I hated the idea of Jetta. There were too many excuses about her.

"Look here, Lucy." Rene turned me around and looked down into my eyes. "You are my business and I'm yours. Jetta *is* going to take no for an answer, if I have to shove it down her throat."

"Please, don't." I pressed my fingers against his lips. "I don't want you using me as your excuse."

"She's hurting *you* now, trying to turn you against me." His lips crushed mine until I felt faint. "I won't lose you."

"Mommy," my little boy said, yawning as he walked into the kitchen. "Are you coming to bed?" Joey was rumpled with sleep. His hair stuck out about his head. His Thomas the Tank pajamas were wrinkled.

"Hey, kiddo," Rene said. He lifted Joey high in his arms.

Joey squealed with delight, touching the ceiling with his fingertips.

"Boy, I never did that before," he said, clinging to Rene's neck.

"I'm going fishing tomorrow and I need a mate to go with me. How's about you and me take the cruiser out to a secret fishing hole and bring home supper?" Rene ruffled Joey's hair.

"Gee whiz, Rene! Can I, Mommy?" Joey turned to me with a wide grin.

I hesitated. Surely Rene would not use Joey to gain my favor? Joey had grown to care for him since they had spent a lot of time together over the last few months.

"What time?" I asked, holding my tirade over Jetta in check to please my son.

"How about six-thirty? And I'll bring lunch." Rene swung Joey around and around, and then put him on the floor. Joey lay there like a beached dolphin, too dizzy to stand.

"Boy, oh boy, wait till I tell Gran!" Joey exclaimed, wiggling around on the floor.

"You better hit the bed and get some sleep, son," said Rene.

"Go on, sweetie. I'll be in to kiss you goodnight." I helped Joey up and patted his bottom.

"Night, Rene. See you tomorrow." Joey skipped out of the room.

"I wish you were coming to my bed and kissing me goodnight," Renee whispered against my lips.

I pushed away. Joey would be waiting. I still couldn't shake the uneasy feeling I had about Jetta.

Rene raised my hand to his mouth and kissed my palm. "Don't let Junior Dykes talk you into another one of his hair-brain schemes. I'd have to hurt him — a lot — if he gets his hands on you again." His tongue stroked my palm and then he was gone.

I heard the cruiser roar to life when he took off for home.

I hurried into Joey's room, but he was already asleep, his cheeks flushed with boyhood dreams.

The next morning Mr. Wilkes and I were busy filling fish orders out on the dock when Rene came and picked up Joey. I kissed them both, deepening my kiss with Rene before slowly releasing him, and then off they went. Joey was glowing with excitement. Gran said she was glad that Joey finally had a prospective father to entertain him. I gave her an innocent smile, but said nothing. I was so sore from lovemaking it took all my concentration to keep up with Mr. Wilkes.

"Miss Lucy, we need to meet with the grabbling committee tomorrow afternoon to go over the rules for this weekend," Mr. Wilkes said, tossing another yellow catfish at me to gut and dress.

"Good Lord, I'd completely forgotten." Junior's crazy manhunts and Rene's pursuit of my affections were making an old lady out of me. I hoped Joey was having a good time today. I wanted Rene in our lives permanently. Sweat dripped from my forehead. The day was going to be a scorcher.

A flicker of movement from the driveway caught my eye, and I looked up to see a female figure walk across the grass and up to the dock gate.

"Lucy?" Leah Ellis stood before me, looking cool and beautiful in a summer suit of pale rose. Her ash-blonde hair framed her heart-shaped face, accented by large gray eyes.

I felt tired, dirty, and ugly in comparison — and with a table full of slimy fish.

"Leah, long time no see." I stood up, smelling her jasmine perfume.

"I really need to talk with you for a few minutes." She leaned into me, pleading with her eyes.

"Let's go sit at the picnic table." I gave Mr. Wilkes a look of frustration, but walked to the wooded table and propped open the umbrella to give us shade. I tossed Leah a cold Coke before swinging my legs across the bench seat.

"It's good of you to give me your time. I know how busy the dock can be in the morning," Leah said, paving the road towards a favor.

"Cut the crap, Leah. What do you want?" I knew I was being a shrew, but Leah showing up like this confirmed the rumors that she and Junior were having an affair.

"You always were one to get to the heart of things, Junior said." She gave me a wry smirk.

"Junior sent you to butter me up?" I popped a Coke top and drank.

"No. He doesn't know I'm here. I came to ask for your help. Junior is feeling very guilty over Sue Ann's death. He was with me that weekend. His father watched the boys while we went to a conference in New Orleans." She was a cool customer.

"I'm not a priest, Leah. Your confession doesn't mean a thing to me." I smashed my Coke can with my fist and then tossed it into the trash.

"Dammit, I'm not confessing. I am worried about Junior. He really hates me now. He keeps coming into my office suggesting I know something about Sue Ann's death. He's even accused me of killing her. I don't want to go to the law, but if he keeps this up, I'll have to protect myself." Her cool armor was dissolving.

"Look, Leah, why don't you take some time off and go visit a relative? I'm sure Sheriff Ware has spoken with you about that night, right?" She nodded. "Well then, I don't see any reason for not taking off."

"The problem is, well, I'm in love with Junior. When we were in New Orleans, he asked me to wait for him while he got a divorce from Sue Ann."

"How long have the two of you been seeing each other?" I was beginning to see the light at the end of the tunnel.

"Going on a year now," she said, fingering her Coke can. "Junior said she could be so awful at times."

"I'm sure you can be pretty awful yourself." I raised an eyebrow at her.

"You must hate me, what with you being an ex-girlfriend and all," Leah said, poison oozing from her lips.

"Leah, this conversation is over. If Junior doesn't want you anymore, there's nothing I can do about it." I stood.

"No, wait. Lucy, I'm sorry. I'm a little jealous of you, I guess. Junior speaks so highly of your family." She had the grace to look embarrassed.

"Go home, Leah." I was exhausted with the conversation.

"Please talk with Junior. He needs to calm down and not be so crazy," she pleaded with me.

Mr. Wilkes cleared his throat. "Miss Lucy, we need to dress these fish before our customers get here."

"Coming, Mr. Wilkes." I rose, eyeing the table full of small catfish.

"I'll say good-bye then," Leah said. She turned toward the gate. The heat had tarnished some of her polish.

Mr. Wilkes and I worked side by side awhile before I asked him, "Now what do you suppose Leah was up to coming here?" I tossed a couple of catfish onto the metal tray.

"I suspect she's protecting her investment." He hefted a thirty-pound catfish to thread a chain through its mouth and then out the gills.

"Junior?" I purported.

"You got it."

"You were right about Junior not being at home when Sue Ann was killed." I tossed the remaining fish onto the tray, wrapped plastic cling film over the meat, and wheeled it to the refrigerator.

"A womanizing husband doesn't make him a killer," Mr. Wilkes commented.

No, but what about his mistress?

CHAPTER THIRTEEN

JUNIOR MOTORED UP TO OUR dock late in the afternoon. I had just finished wrapping Mrs. Jeter's filleted catfish and was waving her good-bye.

Junior jumped onto the dock. He was wearing jean shorts and no shirt. His chest looked rich with black curly hair. He secured his cruiser, with its damaged deck, and then came over to me.

"Lucy." He wrapped his arms around me, lifting me to plant a kiss upon my lips. He deepened the kiss until I struggled to be set free.

"Junior," I push him back. The old Junior use to be a comfort, but this new Junior made me nervous.

Where the hell was Mr. Wilkes?

"Oh, darling, I'm so sorry about last night. I guess Caron brought out the worst in me." He stroked my hair.

Junior's body was solid muscle. I could not break his hold.

"Junior, you don't have a claim on me, so there's nothing to be jealous about," I said, putting him in his place.

"What about college? We were pretty serious until Sue Ann got pregnant. You know I never wanted to marry her. Dad said it was the right thing to do, you know, give the baby my last name." Junior's fingers were kneading my back, his teeth nibbled my neck.

"Junior, what is Leah Ellis going to say about you kissing me?" I shot back. I was beginning to see Junior's true nature, and Sir Galahad he was not.

That got his attention and he finally let me go.

I stepped back and looked around for Mr. Wilkes and saw him stacking buckets.

"Who told you about Leah? Has she been here?" His eyes darkened dramatically. His body mass seemed to increase as his anger intensified.

"I told her," Mr. Wilkes said, walking up to Junior. "Before a man starts accusing others of misdeeds, he needs to look in his own backyard."

Junior seemed to ponder this for a few seconds before he slumped down onto the bench seat of the picnic table. All his anger seemed to seep away.

"Junior, please go home and spend some time with your boys. All this craziness has got to stop." I turned on my heel and headed uphill to the house for lunch.

I showered and change into a clean sundress. It was getting toward evening, and Joey would be home soon. Rene had phoned ahead to say they had enough fish for everyone tonight. I should not be so eager, but God help me, I wanted to spend time with Rene.

I had set the table and was in the process of making fresh brewed tea when Joey, Rene, and Mr. Wilkes entered through the back door. Joey was sunburned about his cheeks. Rene sported a little more color to his bronze body.

"Mommy, look what I caught!" Joey opened the cooler Rene was carrying, and sure enough there were plenty of white perch and brim for everyone.

"I'm so proud of you, honey." I hugged him to me. Fish odor clung to his clothes.

Gran came into the kitchen and Joey had to show off his fish again.

"Hey, little one, let's get you washed and changed while your Mommy fries up your fish," Gran said. She steered Joey to his bedroom. The bruise on her forehead was fading.

"Don't start eating without me," Joey yelled before Gran closed the door on him.

Rene dropped the cooler next to the sink. He smelled good. I guessed he had already showered before leaving the cruiser.

"Miss Lucy, I gotta take Rita to church tonight. They're helping with the grabbling event this weekend." Mr. Wilkes headed for the door. Rita and he had several children by different partners, plus a handful of grandkids. Sometimes they came over to visit us. "See you all in the morning."

"Are you going to meet with the grabbling committee tomorrow?" I asked Rene as I started to wash the fish under the tap water. Rene did a good job of gutting and trimming each fish. I dipped them in cornmeal and dropped them one at a time in the deep fryer.

"Only if you go with me," he said, kissing the back of my neck. Shivers of longing ran down my spine.

"Mr. Wilkes and I will meet you there," I countered his offer. He nipped my ear with his teeth and I yelped.

"Rene, I'm cooking." I gave him a mock protest, but enjoyed his attention.

"What can I do to help you?" he said with a wicked grin while his fingers explored me. I laughed and shook free of his nonsense.

"Hey, stop now. Take that blue platter and layer it with paper towels." I scooped the cracking fish from the fryer and scattered them about the platter. "The tea is ready to put on the table. There's tartar sauce, ketchup, and mustard in the refrigerator. The vinegar is next to the tea container..." And so it went, until the table was ready and we were seated.

Gran bowed her head to say grace. We held hands and prayed to God for our meal. "Amen," we said in unison and then dug in.

Rene was like a native Indian warrior sitting among us. His dark skin heated the kitchen. His blue-black hair was scattered about his shoulders. My fingers itched to touch the thick softness of the strands. Rene caught me staring at him and my cheeks warmed with embarrassment. But Rene didn't laugh. The hunger displayed in his eyes doubled my heartbeat. I tore my glaze from his face and concentrated on eating.

"Mrs. DelRose, I'm very concerned about the river accident." Rene looked at Gran with respect.

"I am, too. That driver was either drunk or crazy. It's a shame they let people like that behind the wheel." Gran scowled.

"Has your insurance company replaced the station wagon?" Rene said, thus including himself as one of our family.

I mulled the idea around in my head a few seconds and decided I wasn't against partnering with Rene at *Rosebud*.

"Lucy and I are going to visit the dealership soon and pick out a new one." Gran wiped tartar sauce from her lips.

"A friend of mine will give you a good deal," Rene said. He and Gran spent the rest of the meal discussing car prices.

After dinner, I walked Rene to the cruiser. He had to get up early in the morning for a meeting regarding a government contract.

"I may be a few minutes late, but I'll see you at the committee meeting," he said, playing with my braid while we stood next to the dock.

I couldn't just let him go without kissing him. He had the same idea, and before I could open my mouth, he was kissing my lips and drawing me against him. All his body warmth transferred to me and I glowed.

"We're going to have to do something about this nighttime stuff," he whispered against my mouth. "Like we go to bed and I wake up with you in my arms."

I didn't know what so say. He hadn't mentioned marriage. Maybe he was one of those guys who didn't believe in it.

As Rene leaned in for another kiss, a gunshot rang out in the night. Rene flung me onto the dock and flattened himself on top of me. I heard a motorboat off in the distance making a run for it.

"Stay down. I'm going after them." Rene jumped on board the cruiser. He started his motors and took to the main channel before I had a rational thought.

Please Lord, watch over him. I was shaking so hard. I raised my head and watched the cruiser fade into the sunset, pursuing the shooter. I dug out my new cell and dialed 911 and told the operator what had occurred. She said she would contact the sheriff's department.

I looked about me. It hadn't been too long since we'd had similar trouble on the dock, and I didn't want to relive that experience. I ran back up the hill to the house and went to my bedroom to change clothes. I took a rifle from the gun cabinet in the library and slipped a few rounds in my pocket.

"Lucy, what's up?" Gran came out of Joey's bedroom.

"Someone shot at us on the dock. Rene went after them. I called 911, but I need to follow Rene." I headed toward the kitchen door.

"Lucy, don't go." She grabbed my arm.

"I need to help Rene." I hugged her gently. I didn't want another invasion of our sanctuary like we'd had a few months back, when security cameras and keypads became a way of life.

Rene burst through the door, saw the rifle in my hand, and took it from me.

"You won't need that right now. I lost the boat on the Louisiana side. The deputies will keep trying, but I think it's impossible." He slung an arm around my shoulders. "Maybe it would be a good idea to activate the cameras and key in your security code."

Gran nodded approval. Rene and I spent forty-five minutes checking all the cameras at the house and dock to make sure they were recording. Next we keyed in the code to activate the security pads in the dock house as well as the main house.

"Rene, I'm so mad. Who is doing this to us?" I moaned against his shoulder.

"I don't know, but I'm working on it." He tightened his arm around my shoulders.

"Why can't people just leave us alone?" My head began to throb. I was beginning to think this was the third clue in Sue Ann's murder.

"Because that cute little nose of yours can't mind its own business." He leaned down and pressed a kiss upon it.

"And what's that suppose to mean?" I stepped back from him.

"Junior Dykes and his murdered wife," Rene said, leaning back against the kitchen door.

"I didn't go after Junior. On the contrary, I've been trying to stop him."

"Junior's unstable. He needs to keep you out of it."

"I feel sorry for him," I admitted softly.

"Look, sweetheart, I know you're trying to help a friend, but the way Junior's going about it is dangerous. He doesn't care where his journey leads him as long as you're there to protect him." Rene took me by the shoulders.

"Protect him?" I was confused.

"From himself. I've heard the rumors about Leah Ellis. He knows he let his wife down. He also let you down nine years ago," Rene whispered this gently, rubbing his hands up and down my arms.

"Me?" That was impossible. I shook my head.

"I've thought about this some. Junior can't correct what he did to Sue Ann, but he can make it right with you. I pretty sure he plans on making you his wife."

"I don't believe it," I said and shook free of him. Upset, I sank down onto a chair at the dining room table.

"I'm worried about his motives. I think if you say *no* to him, he may hurt you." Rene sat down next to me and took my hand.

"Junior wouldn't hurt me." I defended my long time friend.

"Not intentionally, Lucy, but his mind is confused. He married Sue Ann out of obligation."

When I made to argue, he pressed a finger to my lips.

"Yes, I know about Junior, Sue Ann, and you. I'm a native here, you know. Leah isn't the only woman he's had an affair with over the years." He pulled me onto his lap.

"I can't believe this. All these years I assumed their marriage was good. Look at those beautiful boys!" I buried my face against his neck. I seem to be forever misjudging men.

Rene ran his fingers over my hair, and then began loosening the braid. My hair draped us like a curtain. His lips were warm and filled with promise.

After he left for the night, I didn't get much sleep. Junior's boyish charm in college had attracted me. I couldn't make my mind comprehend his change of self.

Junior lurked along the outer marker of my brain as sleep took charge.

CHAPTER FOURTEEN

THE GRABBLING COMMITTEE MET AT the Bayou Restaurant next door to the marina. I walked over with Mr. Wilkes after we sold the last of our fresh fish. The restaurant had a beach motif. We passed lobsters crawling about in a bubbling aquarium. Fake crab claws decorated the walls and staircase as we climbed up to the second floor of the restaurant. Fish nets hung from the ceiling. A waitress outfitted in a blue and white sailor suit directed us to the committee members and other contestants, holed away inside a miniature dining room shaped like a tugboat.

We shook hands with the other contestants and then got down to business. Uncle Royce was present, but Rene had not put in an appearance. The waitress took our orders and we settled down in our seats.

"Okay, boys and girls, looks like we're gonna have another hot grabbling event," announced our chairman, Todd Baker. He was short, bow-legged and bald, but he was a damn good leader. "T.J. checked the winter report this morning. Clear skies through next weekend."

"I'm going to be checking every evening, but it looks like we're okay," T.J. Mann, our co-chairman, confirmed. His carrot-orange hair was blinding.

"We've got men lined up the night before to start building the spectator bleachers and lay the floor for the fish fry," said Brooke Dalton, our promotions go-getter. Brooke was a full-time mom and helped her husband run his sporting goods store in town. She had short, curly brown hair and a cute freckled face.

Trish Kidd, our devoted elderly secretary, never spoke unless it was to clarify a statement for the minutes. She was busy taking notes of the meeting in shorthand.

Cricket Sykes jumped up and ran to a large open box against the wall. Cricket was like her name. She was always leaping from one project to another with a head full of ideas. "See kids, I told you the shirts were awesome!" She held up a simple T-shirt. *Grabbling Competition 2013* was blazed in neon red across the chest and the name of a contestant embossed across the back.

"Royce, you and your nephew will have your T-shirts in a couple of days," Cricket assured him. "We had to put a rush on it." No one mentioned the reason for the rush: that Junior's team T-shirts had to be replaced.

Rene walked in during the middle of the T-shirt demonstration. He shook hands all around and then sat next to Royce, giving me a wink.

My cheeks became warm.

Our seafood arrived and we ate while going over the rules of the contest. Rene and Royce kept talking in hushed tones throughout the meal. Todd glanced a time or two, but didn't admonish them.

Mr. Wilkes said in a low voice, "I think this is going to be our best year."

I patted his hand and nodded.

After two hours, we broke, agreeing to arrive early on Saturday to make ready for the event.

"Lucy," Rene called out to me as I started to follow Mr. Wilkes out.

I stopped and let him catch up. Royce and Mr. Wilkes went on ahead.

"Any trouble last night?" His thumb stroked my palm. His touch made me all gooey inside.

"No," I said. I didn't want Rene to know I'd lain awake all night.

"I'm sending a man over today to watch the monitors." His tone brooked no argument.

"As long as he stays inside the dock house," I said, squirming under Rene's touch.

"Done." He pressed his lips against my wrist.

I drank in the way his jeans stretched taut across his bulge. The polished cotton shirt strained at the button holes that covered hard biceps. His black hair was secured at the base of his neck with one of my blue ribbons.

"Tomorrow I want us to take a practice run at the barrels." He turned me around and then leaned down so that we were in our own quiet space. "I want you to go over that territory until you can see it with your eyes closed. With all the crazies out there again, we need to be very careful." He took me by the chin and dropped a kiss on my mouth.

I knew he was worried. Maybe this was how he showed his love for me, keeping me safe.

"Okay, but I want Mr. Wilkes there to walk it with me, since we're partners," I reasoned.

"Deal," he said and sealed it with another kiss.

I started down the stairs with Rene leading the way. Suddenly the steps seem to be moving and I stumbled and fell headfirst into Rene, knocking him off balance. We both ended up at the bottom of the steps.

"Are you okay?" Rene jumped to his feet. He helped me up.

"I'll live." My head hurt a little from the jarring fall, but it wasn't worth mentioning. I dusted off my jeans.

A uniformed waitress came downstairs. She was holding a broken drinking glass.

"This was on the stairs. I can't understand how it got there." She handed it over to the manager, who had come running up at the commotion.

"I'm terribly sorry, folks," he said, hovering over us. "Please accept my apologies."

"We're fine. Lucy, come on." Rene took my arm and guided me outside into the afternoon heat.

"Lucy, I hate to leave you, but I must get back to the shop. I'll call you later today." He went over to join Royce, and they drove off in a white Chevrolet pickup truck.

Mr. Wilkes and I walked back to the marina. Gran met us at the dock.

"Joey wants to visit Junior's boys," she said.

"That could be a problem, Gran. Junior's been chasing after the people Sue Ann saw during the last few weeks of her life. He's on some kind of guilt trip over her death." I flung out my hands in exasperation.

"I'll get Mack to bring the boys over today," Gran said, patting my arm."Junior doesn't have to come. He should be at the feed store."

"Okay, Gran." I gave up, kissed her check, and then joined Mr. Wilkes. We loaded the runabout for a trip downriver to check out our nets. We were about to leave when a young man in shop uniform showed up. He introduced himself as Rene's employee, Wilson Woodson, and said Rene had sent him over to watch the security monitors. I showed Wilson the back room of the dock house and he settled in.

"Y'all be careful now," Gran yelled out at us.

"Stay close to the house," I urged her. "Remember, the walls have eyes now."

"I'll remember." Gran gave me a salute and headed back uphill to the house to greet Mack and his grandkids.

Gran was a trip. Nothing fazed her.

Mr. Wilkes and I headed downriver. I captained the *Little Mermaid* into the main channel, past Turtle Island, and then worked our way among the reeds to drift up to our hiding place. The net was submerged in about four feet of water. Mr. Wilkes grasped the hinged lid at one end and I took weight at the other. Tiny holes in the mesh net where I could dig in my fingers and get a good grasp allowed me to easily retrieve it and lift it inside the boat. Fish trapped within the net thrashed about inside.

Heat bore down upon us as we shook the net free of fish, turtles — and a pink baby dolphin about the size of my son.

"Mr. Wilkes! I've never seen a river dolphin this far north." I gently scoped up the squirming mammal, gauging the calf's weight at about sixty pounds. Mr. Wilkes used his cell phone to take a picture of me holding the bottlenose dolphin.

"We need to put him back in the river, Miss Lucy." Mr. Wilkes continued empting the net.

"Maybe we should call the museum to have them take care of him." I dipped a towel into the water and then wrapped the dripping cloth against the dolphin's rubbery skin. I patted and held him gently.

"I'm not sure his mother ain't out there pining for her calf?" Mr. Wilkes scanned the area.

"You think we should release him?" I hugged the little dolphin to me, forever the protective mother.

"His mother has to be around here."

"Could be he went looking for her and got caught in the net."

Mr. Wilkes shrugged.

"Let's call Gerdie at the museum right now," I said. Gerdie Parish was a marine biologist at the wildlife museum in Jackson. I flipped opened my cell phone and made the call. Gerdie was thrilled at our find. She would leave right away with a container to pick him up and gave us instructions on protecting him until she could arrive. I cushioned the dolphin's body with life-preservers and draped him with wet towels, keeping him shaded while we motored back to the marina with over fifty fish flapping their tails at us and one pink dolphin nestled in the bow.

We rode in on our own waves and slid into the dock slip. Mr. Wilkes pressed the button to lift the runabout out of the water. I poured more water over the dolphin, then helped Mr. Wilkes unload the fish into the wooden crate to clean in the morning.

"Mommy, a dolphin!" My son jumped up and down on the dock.

"Don't scare him," I warned and led Joey to the boat.

When Joey extended his hand to touch him, the dolphin made a clear, high pitched announcement that knocked Joey on his rump with surprise. The dolphin let out another request. Joey scampered out of the boat.

"Mommy, something is wrong with him," Joey said, grabbing my arm.

"No, honey, he's just a baby and frightened." I hugged Joey to me. "Let me pour more water on him." I dropped back into the boat and slowly emptied a pail of river water over the little calf.

A commotion at the gate announced Gerdie Parish hustling through with two other marine biologists. Gerdie was a prematurely gray-haired lady with horn-rim glasses and a smile as wide as Texas. Her colleagues were male and on the young side.

"Lucy, good to see you." Gerdie clasped me by the shoulders in a bear hug. "Let me look at this adorable pink angel." She eased down into the boat, joined by her male counterparts.   Within thirty minutes, they had the dolphin transferred into a mobile container with enough water to keep him alive for the trip to the museum.

Gran wandered out from the dock house. When she saw the pink dolphin, her eyes widened in surprise.

"Where did you get this little darling?"

I explained our discovery while Gran and the others listened attentively.

"Lucy, you guys can visit anytime," Gerdie said. "This little albino dolphin will be a hit with the kids at the museum."

"Mommy, let's go visit tomorrow," Joey piped up.

"Well, Joey, not so soon," Gerdie told him. "We'll need to get an exhibit tank ready for him to settle him in. Maybe a couple of weeks." She tousled Joey's blond hair.

"Thanks for coming so quick, Gerdie." I walked with her to their van.

"No problem. We'll need to get this guy to the museum." Gerdie hugged me again.

I waved good-bye to the other guys.

"Mommy, he's so cool." Joey gave me a hug.

CHAPTER FIFTEEN

I SLIPPED INTO THE MUDDY water of the Mississippi River, with Mr. Wilkes bringing up my rear. The sun shone brightly and lit up our underwater theatre of dancing reeds and red blanket of mud. This was a clear site for the barrels, with no heavy debris to mar this area for the grabbling event. Mr. Wilkes and I swam underwater among the barrels while Rene stayed above us in the runabout. All six barrels were spread out about forty foot apart along the bend at the river. Tree trunks shielded a couple of them, making it an ideal hiding place for flat-head catfish. I looked over at Mr. Wilkes. He nodded, and we kicked our way back up to the surface.

"Well, how'd it look?" Rene hung over the side of the boat, his long black hair blowing in the morning breeze. He wore his usual tan work shirt.

"Why don't you come down and see for yourself?" Mr. Wilkes asked.

"Clear back." Rene tossed his shirt off and then shucked his pants in less than five seconds, revealing black boxer shorts. He flipped backward off the runabout, much like scuba divers I'd seen on television.

Even though the grabbling event was a competition, each team was allowed to check out the site to familiarize themselves with the location of the barrels. There was no guarantee a catfish would be inside one during the actual event. That was the prize factor.

I climbed up the stern ladder and watched Mr. Wilkes and Rene move about below. I was just thinking how mild the river traffic was this morning, when all of the sudden a speedboat careened around the turn and headed straight for me. The fiberglass boat glittered red in the sunlight, and the harsh glare kept me from identifying the pilot. I was terribly worried about Rene and Mr. Wilkes a few feet below me, but I didn't have time to raise the anchor, so I did the only thing I could think of.

I jumped overboard, landing on top of Rene. Mr. Wilkes turned toward us just as the speedboat's propeller blades stirred the water into a muddy stew. The impact to the runabout was brutal. Ripping metal could be heard, even underwater.

Rene shoved me away from the whirling propeller blades. I landed on the reeds near shore alongside Mr. Wilkes and crawled along the riverbank as quickly as I could until my head was above water. Looking over my shoulder, I saw Rene climb into the damaged runabout, lift anchor, and start the engine. The speedboat had reversed. I could make out the pilot now: a figure in green coveralls, sporting a cap pulled low over the forehead.

"I'm damned if we just lost another boat," Mr. Wilkes said. He climbed up to join me on the riverbank.

The speedboat flew across the river and into the main channel. Rene kicked ass pursuing it.

"Someone really wants us dead," I said, rubbing the water from my eyes.

"Not *us*, Ms. Lucy. They want to kill you." Mr. Wilkes pulled out his white handkerchief, now brown with mud.

"I stopped helping, Junior," I replied indignantly.

"Doesn't matter. You started out with him. The killer may think you know enough to make it worthwhile seeing you dead." Mr. Wilkes eased up further along dry land.

"Hell, what's the use of having friends if I can't help them?" I said stubbornly.

"Not in a murder case." Mr. Wilkes raised his voice.

I mulled this over and knew he was right. I should have stayed out of it and let the law handle the witnesses. If I'd realized how much Junior had changed from the man I knew in college, I would have declined.

The crippled runabout reappeared off the horizon. Rene eased up to the bank, trimming the prop out of the water. He'd put his work clothes back on and tied my blue ribbon at the nape of his neck.

"Get in. I'll take y'all home." Rene was subdued. He stood behind the console, avoiding our eyes.

"What's up, Rene?" I stood next to him and suddenly noticed the ugly red cut dripping blood from his right arm. "You're hurt."

Mr. Wilkes hoisted the first-aid kit out of the bow compartment and quickly went about cleaning and dressing the wound. I used one of my scarves as a makeshift sling for Rene's arm. Rene took the discomfort like a pro.

"Tell us about the speedboat, Rene," I would brook no argument. I cupped his face within the palms of my hands and made him look at me. "What happened?"

"The speedboat ran aground next to Turtle Island. The pilot made a dash for the woods. I gave chase, but fell into a bore trap and cut my arm on the spikes. By the time I climbed out, the guy was gone and so was the boat."

"Thank God you weren't hurt worse." I hugged him to me. I could tell he was holding something back, but I didn't press. Rene knew more about the pilot than he was willing to share. By the look on Mr. Wilkes face, he suspected the same thing.

Rene dropped us off at DelRose Marina Dock and promised to have another boat delivered until the *Little Mermaid* could be repaired.

He wrapped his good arm around me and held me tight against him. The warmth of his body heated my cheek. His skin smelled sunburned.

"Are you going to be able to grabble with this arm?" I asked, worried about his injury.

"Don't worry, little mermaid. I'll grabble with my toes if I have to," he chuckled.

I'd never heard him chuckle before. It was kind of sexy.

"I radioed the sheriff about the speedboat," Rene went on. "He's going to meet me at shop before coming over here to talk to you."

Gran came out of the dock house and did a double-take when she saw the damage to our new runabout.

"What happened?" she said.

Rene filled her in, then he took off into the main channel, heading south.

"Lucy, the boys are in the dock house helping me clean. You and Mr. Wilkes finish up while I go and put together lunch."

"Yes, Gran." I never argued with her. The clues in this case were beginning to add up. The killer must think I knew more than I did about Sue Ann's murder. Actually, I knew next to nothing.

I found Junior's boys mopping the floor and Joey wiping down counters and tables. The boys were really good sports. We finished and headed up the hill. I needed a shower and clean clothes.

Mr. Wilkes looked in on Wilson, the guard Rene had sent, before using the dock house bathroom to shower and change.

"Mommy, what happened to our boat?" Joey had overheard my conversation with Gran.

"A speedboat ran into it," I didn't elaborate, not wanting him to tell Junior's boys the news.

"Is Rene going to fix it?" Joey wanted to know.

"You bet," I said and headed for the bathroom. Twenty minutes later, I entered the kitchen. Smells of cooking fish and French fries made my mouth water.

After lunch Mr. Mack arrived to pick up his grandsons. He pulled Gran aside and had words with her before leaving.

"Mack said Junior took off a few hours ago and no one knows where he went," Gran told me after he left. She wiped down the dining table.

A few minutes later, Sheriff Ware showed up at our back door. I gave him a glass of iced tea and we went out to sit on the porch.

"Miss DelRose, we need to compare notes." Sheriff Ware dug in his shirt pocket and took out a notepad, then tossed his gray felt hat on the wicker chair next to him.

"First, you and your grandmother are forced off the road and into the river. Second, Junior takes you to an old camp site, and then a speedboat crashes into you. Did I leave anything out?" He had been checking off each item.

"Only that Leah Ellis paid me a visit yesterday. She wanted me to calm Junior down. Said he accused her of killing Sue Ann." I hated putting Junior on the spot.

"I knew Junior and Leah Ellis were running around, but I didn't know he had turned on her." Ware wrote in his notepad. "Do you have any idea who was operating the speedboat?"

"None," I said, shaking my head.

"Are you still participating in the grabbling event this weekend?" He pocketed his notepad.

"Yes, of course." I stood up.

"Be careful." Sheriff Ware left the porch and climbed into his squad car.

Being careful wasn't in my nature. I couldn't help but wonder where Junior was keeping himself.

CHAPTER SIXTEEN

I WAS AWAKENED BY THE sound of footsteps. Someone was walking on the porch outside my bedroom window. I sat up in bed and watched shadows play across the wisps of curtain paneling. Quickly as I could, I exited the bedroom and made for the library, where I had security monitors fed into the outside cameras. Sure enough, the camera picked up a man walking along the porch to the back of the house. His face was shadowed by a wide brim hat pulled low to cover most of his face. I punched in the dock house number and Wilson picked up. He was watching the stranger as well.

"I put a call into my boss and dialed 911. Stay inside. Do you have your keypad code punched in?" Wilson said.

"Yes," I replied.

"Then all hell's going to break loose if he tries to enter the house." Wilson hung up.

I continued to watch the stranger. He did try to open the backdoor, but gave up when he found it locked, and left the house, heading downhill toward the dock. Wilson had better be ready for him. The stranger was a big guy with brawny shoulders. I started to return to my bedroom to dress, but the wall phone rang.

"Yes?" I said.

"Don't even think about going outside." Rene's calm voice settled my nerves. "I'm coming up next to Bayou Restaurant. I see him on the dock. He's got a boat. I'm going to hold back and follow him."

"Be careful." My voice trembled.

"Always." Rene disconnected.

I stayed and watched the scene play out. The stranger dropped into a small runabout and took off upriver. After a few seconds, Rene's cruiser followed, showing no running lights. As I stood looking out the window, a deputy car pulled up next to the house. I hurried to the kitchen door, keyed in the code, and opened the door to Deputy Griggs.

"The trespasser just left by boat, headed upriver," I told him. "Rene Caron is following in a cruiser." I reported the rest of the story and promised to keep a copy of the security tape for the sheriff. I watched the deputy step back into his patrol car and leave.

I turned back toward the kitchen door and was grabbed from behind. A man's hand clamped down across my mouth.

"It's about freaking time," Junior growled into my ear.

He pulled me backward toward the front of the house. I struggled hard against his hands.

Suddenly Wilson jumped over the porch rail and attacked Junior. Junior cold-cocked him in the jaw and he crumbled on the porch. Junior's left hand never released my wrist.

"I'll hurt you, Lucy, if you don't settle down. I'm going to complete this investigation and find Sue Ann's killer." He sounded angry and crazy at the same time.

I went limp. I'd be damned if I made it any easier on him. Junior swore under his breath before lifting me and tossing me across his shoulder like a sack of potatoes. At least my mouth was free, but I didn't want to scream and scare Gran and Joey.

Junior dumped me inside a Bronco truck and shoved me across the cushioned bench seat.

"Junior, how can I help you if you keep scaring me?" I knew my voice sounded strained, but I was tired of this game.

"You're some friend. At first you were all for helping. What happened? Your new boyfriend told you to lay off?" He ground the gears of the standard shift and then pulled out into the night.

"Why can't you let law enforcement find Sue Ann's killer?" I said, tugging at my baby-doll pajamas to cover my ass. At least I had thought to slip on the matching robe. My hair was a tangle down my back.

"Lucy, I let her down once. I can't do it again," he said, his voice forlorn. He drove like a robot on autopilot.

I wanted to reach out to Junior in his moment of grief, but I knew it would only encourage his madness. A few seconds later, a buzzing sensation against my thigh had me nearly jumping out of my skin. I realized I had my cell phone in my robe pocket. I causally adjusted my robe and managed to press the talk button.

"Junior, where are you taking me?" I eased back against the truck seat.

"We're going to where Sue Ann was killed." He said it like we were on our way to a picnic.

"Out on that deserted road?" A tremor was in my voice. I was getting a bad feeling here.

"I found her handbag and a scarf this evening when I was at the feed store, you know, back of the warehouse. Remember that hippie we saw at the Blue Bird Bar & Grill? He met her back there to give her drugs." Junior's face was like stone.

"Junior, Sue Ann was killed in the truck." I combed my fingers through my hair. This was getting creepier and creepier.

"I got a feeling about him," he continued as if I hadn't said a word. "He was always touching her, laughing at some joke, hanging around. It's got to be him." Junior ground the gearshift to neutral as we pulled up to a red light.

"Why not tell Sheriff Ware or Sheriff Umbridge? It's their job to know these things." I tried to reason with him.

"To hell with them. No one wants to listen." The light turned green and we drove along the highway on our way toward Rolling Fork.

"What good is it to go to the feed store tonight? You need the sheriff to gather the evidence you found, not me." I humored him. I combed my fingers through my hair again. My nerves were in overdrive.

"I want to show you myself where Sue Ann's things were found. So you can see that she wouldn't have left her purse behind. The sheriff is mistaken about where she was killed."

I'd just opened my mouth to comment when the Bronco was rammed violently from behind. The impact sent us sailing forward. I almost went through the windshield, but grabbed the dash rail.

"Dear God, hold on. Here he comes again!" I screamed. We were rammed even harder than before. The Bronco did a tail-spin and flipped over the median into a deep trench. Junior fell on top of me. The motor revved and the wheels were still spinning on their axles. I smelled gas fumes. *Dear God, please help us out of this mess.* Junior's body was dead weight. I heaved and struggled, but I couldn't budge him. I began to cry in frustration.

"Lucy!" Rene's voice was somewhere above me.

"Rene, help. Junior's on top of me. I can't move." I was having difficulty breathing.

More voices surrounded the upside-down Bronco. The jaws-of-life tore at my door, ripping it from its hinges. Rescuers reached in and pulled us out of the Bronco.

Rene gathered me against him. His face was grim and covered with mud. He carried me to his truck, where he shook out a blanket and wrapped the soft material around me. I was a mess. My pajamas and robe were mud-streaked and my hair was tangled. I pressed my face against Rene. I felt him shudder and I clung to him, letting the tears come. My neck ached from whiplash.

Rene slipped in next to me on the truck seat. Next thing I knew he gathered me up onto his lap. I winced when he tightened his grip. I was sore all over. Kisses rained across my cheeks and forehead, soothing my nerves.

"Let's get you to the emergency room and have you checked out," Rene mumbled against my neck.

I nodded, too emotionally charged to speak.

"I saw that blue Dodge ram you. I would have chased him down, but I knew we had to get you two out of there." His voice was raw with emotion.

"Miss DelRose, are you hurt?" Sheriff Ware broke in on our intimate moment. Sirens screamed behind him while we remained isolated in a world of our own.

"I just hurt all over." I snuggled closer in the protection of Rene's arms. He tightened his hold.

"What happened?" The sheriff took out his notepad and began writing while I told my story.

"I think that blue Dodge truck was the same one that shoved us into the river."

"You sure?"

"I can't swear to it in court, but it looked like the same truck."

"Then someone is following either you or Junior." Sheriff Ware snapped his notepad closed. "It's beginning to look like the two of you have stumbled across evidence that is making the killer nervous."

I told him about Junior's discovery of Sue Ann's purse and scarf at the feed store. I also told him that Junior didn't believe Sue Ann was killed inside the truck.

"We have proven to him that she was killed inside the truck. I'll question him about it."

"I'm taking Lucy to the hospital." Rene eased me off his lap and he slid behind the steering wheel. The motor rumbled to life. Sheriff Ware closed the passenger door and waved us through the accident scene.

"So, Junior is ready to take you down with him trying to find his wife's killer." Rene said it more like a statement than a question.

"Something is definitely wrong with Junior," I said. "He's never been like this before." I sank deeper into the soft blanket.

"Lucy, I don't want you near him." Rene eased the truck into the stream of southbound traffic.

The hospital was busy, but Rene managed to get me seen by emergency staff. I had bruises on my arms and legs and had suffered a whiplash, but nothing serious. I was glad when the doctor gave me a pill to ease my pain and a prescription for muscle relaxers to help my neck. The nurse gave me a cotton wrap to cover my pajamas. Rene walked me back to his truck and helped me up into the seat.

I rested against the truck seat and closed my eyes, enjoying the rumble of the diesel engine vibrating my body. I must have fallen asleep because the next thing I knew Rene was lifting me in his arms. He walked to the back door and gently set me on my feet.

"No one knows you left the house," he whispered against my ear.

"Is Wilson okay?" I suddenly remembered the security guard.

"Yes, but his jaw will hurt for a spell. Junior's got a powerful right punch." Rene's forehead creased into a frown.

"I need to get some sleep. Gran will want a full report in the morning. If she hears about this through the grapevine, my goose is cooked." I took his hand in mine.

"I want you to put a restraining order out on Junior. He's going to get you killed if he keeps this up," Rene said, cupping my face within his callused palms. He leaned down and pressed a kiss upon my lips. I sighed, my needs awakening.

"I'll check with Wilson to make sure no one else has been hanging around." He shoved me inside the kitchen door. "Punch in the security code," he ordered.

I quickly set the code and then watched him walk down to the dock house.

My life just kept getting more and more dangerous.

CHAPTER SEVENTEEN

RACHEL BECKER AND I MOVED through the underbrush on the trail of a mechanical deer she had plugged several yards back. Rachel blended with the wildlife in camouflage pants and T-shirt with a matching cap. I was dressed similarly. Rachel had called me early this morning with an offer to target practice before I began dressing fish. Junior's kidnapping rendition could wait until later that day. Gran was asleep when I left the house at four-thirty. I penned a note and swallowed a muscle relaxer to get me through the day.

Turtle Island was set up with mechanical deer, turkeys, and squirrels for target practice. The animals were mounted on moving rails to make them more realistic.

Dawn broke over the treetops to the east. Wildlife had put up a racket during our hike through the woods. Calm descended over me when I cleared the underbrush and saw the deer target, partially hidden by an oak tree. I was in my element. I aimed at the deer with my .30-06 rifle and squeezed off a shot to the head. The bullet hit its mark and the deer took off on its rail.

"Good shot, Lucy," Rachel gave me a pat on the shoulder. I reloaded and hit the trail again.

"Now if we do as well during hunting season, we'll have some venison to eat." I said. I had a hard time keeping up with Rachel. She ate up the trail with her long legs.

"Hey, ready for a breakfast break?" Rachel came to a halt and sat down on a tree trunk. Her mood swings drive me crazy.

I wedged in next to her, and we enjoyed the blueberry muffins she'd packed in her knapsack. We had bottled water to wash them down.

"How's Junior holding up after last night's accident?" Rachel commented casually. She wiped the sweat from her brow with a handkerchief.

I knew she was picking her way at a story, but I kept my tone light.

"Last I heard, he was fine." I bit off another mouthful of muffin. Junior had spent the night at the hospital for observation.

"You know, Junior is kind of a playboy." Rachel peeked at me from under her long lashes. I had always envied her model's slim face and hollow cheeks.

"I can't see him finding the time," I countered. I felt an obligation to protect Junior's reputation. There were his three sons to consider and the memory of their mother.

"I don't want to spread rumors; I only want to get to the bottom of who killed Sue Ann."

"Then investigate the crime, not the husband."

"How can I separate the two? Witnesses say Sue Ann was distraught over Junior's roving eye." Rachel licked blueberries from her fingers.

The blueberries tasted heavenly, and I licked my fingertips, too, appreciating the quiet around us. A squirrel circled a tree trunk before spreading his legs to leap to another tree. The frogs croaked from a small pond off to our left. I love the forest. Hunting game was nature's way of reminding us how it was before civilization.

"Rachel, just don't go after Junior because he's a womanizer. Get to the meat of this case. Why did Sue Ann have to die?" I dusted the crumbs from my jeans and stood up.

"Isn't that what you and Junior have been working on?" she retorted.

"No. We have been retracing her steps the last few weeks, but not coming up with much. The law seems to be making progress, but Junior keeps pulling at the bit."

"Come let me show you the trailer I had hauled into camp last month." Rachel hooked my left arm and pulled me down a trail further east. After a few minutes, the woods opened to a circle of nice camping trailers and a huge fire pit. I liked it. The camp was clean and well tended. A bigger trailer with yellow awning and a wooden porch was set up at the end of the circle.

"Looks good," I said, nodding my approval.

"I want you to be my guest when hunting season opens." Rachel hugged my arm to her body.

I patted her hand. Rachel was a good hunting partner. I could trust her with guns and ammo. She was a safe sportsman.

"I can't wait, Rachel."

"Oh, I meant to tell you — I'll be covering the grabbling event this weekend."

"That's great," I said. I slipped my rifle over my shoulder and readjusting my knapsack.

"I understand that you and Rene Caron are a hot item." Rachel gave me one of her knowing looks.

"Rachel, I wish you'd get married and have a houseful of kids. You need something to keep your mind busy," I said and playfully pushed her off-balance.

"If you hang with Rene, it's you who will have a houseful of children," she said and pushed back.

I blushed, avoiding Rachel's probing eyes. My feelings for Rene were still too new and I was vulnerable to outside opinions.

"Okay, come on let's get back to the boat." Rachel reached across me for her knapsack she had tossed next to the fire pit. A shot rang out and Rachel fell against me, knocking us to the ground. Dirt few up around us. Another shot followed, ricocheting off the new trailer.

I dragged Rachel's dead weight behind the fire pit and swung my rifle up to scope out the woods behind the campers. The underbrush rustled and I squeezed off a shot.

"Rachel, you okay?" I said without looking at her. I kept my eye trained on the woods through the rifle scope.

"Yeah, but my shoulder hurts like hell fire," she said, gasping.

"Keep on the ground. I think I may have hit him, but I'm not sure." The underbrush moved again, but further off. I wanted to track the shooter, but I couldn't leave Rachel.

"Are they gone?" she mumbled.

I looked down and saw blood staining her T-shirt. I knelt and pulled back the T-shirt from her shoulder. There was an entrance wound and an exist wound. Good. The bullet was somewhere on the ground.

"Is there a first-aid kit in your trailer?" I had her by the waist and hefted her weight. Sweat poured off me from the strain of keeping it together for Rachel's safety. Thankfully, she managed to walk without passing out. Rachel might be slim, but she was a lot of woman.

"Yeah, in the bathroom," she said.

I shouldered my rifle and made for the trailer entrance. There were no further shots.

Rachel handed me the trailer key and I had us inside and her on the couch in record time. I used the first-aid kit to stop the flow of blood and clean the wound. My hands shook. I knew the bullet was meant for me. If Rachel hadn't leaned across me at that exact moment, it would have struck me in the chest. Rachel had saved my life.

The Bubba in Sue Ann's murder was a busy guy.

I pulled out my cell phone and called Mr. Wilkes, explaining the situation. I asked him to call the sheriff's office and then come and get us. Rachel needed to go to the hospital.

An hour later, we had Bunge County law enforcement at the campsite. Deputy Griggs found the bullet that exited Rachel's shoulder. Mr. Wilkes helped me load her into our borrowed runabout and we made for DelRose Dock.

"Miss Lucy, you nearly lost your life back there," Mr. Wilkes said quietly to me while Rachel lay back against the cushioned seats.

"I know. This guy is serious about eliminating witnesses." I stepped closer to Mr. Wilkes, like his body could protect me.

"I think it's time you went back into hiding," he said, trimming down the prop as we slid next to our dock. Mr. Wilkes eased the runabout onto our boat slip and pushed the button that raised the boat out of the water.

An ambulance was waiting to take Rachel to the hospital, and I rode with her.

The hospital was busy, but Rachel was whisked into X-ray in record time. The doctors gave her an injection for pain before they cleaned the wound and redressed it. The nurse also gave her a tetanus shot for infection and a sling to keep her shoulder from moving. After setting up an appointment with her doctor for the following day, Rachel was released in my care.

A deputy drove us back to Rosebud, where Gran fussed over Rachel and put her to bed in the guestroom.

Once Rachel was settled, Sheriff Ware sat down with me in the kitchen. Gran followed us in, and got out the iced tea.

"Didn't see the shooter?" he said.

"No, only the underbrush moving as he got away." I accepted a glass of tea from Gran. Sheriff Ware declined her offer with a shake of his head.

"You've made this guy really nervous," the sheriff said. He ran a hand over his bare head. His gray felt hat rested on one of the dining chairs.

"I don't see how. I haven't talked with anyone else about this case," I said.

"I wonder if you and Junior made contact with the killer that night at the Blue Bird Bar & Grill?" he said, retrieving his hat.

"The only person Junior talked with was the hippie guy," I reminded him.

"I know, but did you speak to anyone after we went out into the street?" he said.

"I followed the hippie to the telephones when he made a phone call," I said and told the sheriff about Bubba.

"Bubba," he said the name like a sore in his mouth.

"Yes," I nodded.

"Miss DelRose, you are a champion at keeping information from me," he scolded.

"I honestly thought I'd told you." I felt bad.

"Well it looks like Ricky Downs has more to tell me about Sue Ann," he said.

"Is Ricky the hippie?"

"Yes, he is. Oh, I forgot to tell you that we found a blood trail. It ended at the river's edge. Looks like you hit your target."

I wonder if it was Bubba?

CHAPTER EIGHTEEN

R ENE CARON'S APARTMENT WAS A wet dream. Nestled in the back corner of his massive welding shop, the apartment was equipped with a fully functioning kitchen decorated in hunter green counter tiles, custom cedar cabinets, and a black and white tiled floor. The living area was comfortably furnished with deep-cushioned chairs and sofa. The white plush carpet accented the stone fireplace and the black bear rug. Lamps with soft lighting cast a mysterious aura about the room.

Rene had left a message on my cell phone to meet him here for lunch. It was more of a command. He probably wanted to give me a lecture about the shooting. Rene was getting worse than Mr. Wilkes at bossing me around.

Royce let me into the apartment. "Rene will be with you shortly. He's finishing up with a client." He tipped his cap at me before departing.

I entered the kitchen, appreciating the stack of fried catfish and cold slaw waiting to be eaten. Someone had gone through the trouble of setting the table and brewing fresh tea.

I was wearing a blue sundress and white sandals, and my hair swung about my waist. I went to check out the office monitors to see if Rene was heading this way. Then the back door opened and Rene stepped inside, his bronze skin shiny with sweat. His black hair was tied back with a leather strip. Work pants and shirt clung to his damp skin. He kissed me lightly on the mouth.

"Let me jump into the shower," he said and disappeared into the bedroom.

I knew Joey would be disappointed that I hadn't brought him along. He loved Rene's apartment. Gran and Mr. Wilkes would open the dock house after lunch, and Joey was going to help wrap the fish purchases.

Suddenly the back door banged opened and I experienced déjà vu. The temperature in the hallway dropped to a chilly breeze when Jetta Angelo charged through, dressed in her usual gypsy clothing of ruffles and peasant blouse. Her alabaster skin emphasized the redness of her lips and the slant of her eyes. Her body glittered with bracelets, bangles, and earrings, her long fingernails dripped with blood red polish. Her raven hair was teased about her face. Dark eyes shot daggers at me. But what had me shaking inside was the bandage wrapped around her upper arm. Blood had seeped out of the wound and soaked the dressing. My eyes bore into hers. I could feel the hate radiating toward me. I didn't say a word.

"Stay away from Rene," she warned me with a deadly stare. She stepped closer, looking down at me from her added height.

"Back off," I hissed. I wouldn't give her the satisfaction of seeing me scared.

"He's just after that pussy of yours," she said, venom oozing with each word. She slammed out of the apartment, but not before Rene saw her. He drew the deadbolt on the backdoor.

"Sorry about Jetta," he said.

"Why is she here all the time?" I said. Jetta's bandaged arm set off alarms in my head. Was she the shooter?

"Jetta is like a shadow. She sneaks around the shop, but we have a hard time catching her." Rene ran his fingers up and down my arms.

"You have security here. Why does she get past it?" I didn't believe that Jetta was history. She still had the run of the place.

"She knows where the cameras are hidden."

"Rene, I can't come here anymore," I said.

He pushed me up against the kitchen wall, then leaned down and kissed me with such hunger, I swooned.

"Don't say that, even in jest." He gathered me up in his arms and took me to the living room, settling us onto the sofa with me on his lap.

"Rene, I'm not jesting. Jetta makes it plain that you belong to her. I haven't heard you deny it." I slid off his lap. Rene pulled me back.

"I broke up with Jetta more than a year ago. She became obsessive with our relationship. I was never committed to her."

"To some women, the mere fact you are having sex with them is enough of a commitment." I reasoned.

"Is that what you think?" He ran his fingers through my hair.

"As far as we are concerned, sex would be a commitment," I said. It was one of the reasons I could relate to Jetta and her obsessive behavior.

Rene turned my face to his and stared down at me with a wounded expression.

"I am committing to you. I want to be able to offer you and Joey a home with a yard, flowers, marina, you know, everything you have with your grandmother. I'm working hard to make that happen. You mean the world to me. When I think of someone shooting at you...." He trailed off, his voice breaking a little.

I trembled. Rene was sensitive to my needs as he had already demonstrated when I went into the river in my car. I wrapped my arms around my strong Indian warrior and hugged him to me, pressing my lips to the side of his neck, so warm and inviting. Rene's hands roamed my body, and he lay back against the cushions, bringing me with him. The morning's shooting scare began to fade.

Rene was breathing hard. He rolled off me, pulling me on top of him. I lay with my face buried into his chest, purring like a kitten. My limbs were loose and I was floating on a cloud of pleasure. My eyelids fluttered, feeling secure, I fell to sleep.

"Little mermaid…" Rene's husky voice penetrated my conscious. "Time to get up." He nipped my shoulder with his teeth.

I squirmed around on top of him. I was warm and comfortable. The sofa was a haven for my fears. Protesting, I moaned and settled deeper against Rene's muscular body. Husky laughter rumbled against my ear and I grinned at the implication.

A few minutes later we ate cold catfish and drank sweet tea.

"I'm scared about these near misses that you keep having," Rene said, swallowing a mouthful of fish.

"Well, I'm not looking for trouble," I told him. "Rachel and I were target practicing on Turtle Island. No one knew we were going until we set foot in the runabout and headed over." I sipped more tea.

"Someone is watching you. Don't go anywhere alone." He leaned forward and kissed me.

I smiled, loving the feel of his lips upon mine.

We left the apartment about thirty minutes later and walked down the pier to a smaller runabout he had loaned me until the *Little Mermaid* was repaired.

"Wilson will be back on duty tonight as security guard at the dock house," he reminded me.

"Who's minding the store now?" I leaned into him.

"Royce went over earlier," Rene said, stroking my hair.

I heard the rifle shot as it echoed among the trees to be swallowed by the river in the late afternoon sun. Rene threw me down on the pier, covering my body with his. Suddenly the thud of running feet headed our way from the shop. Shouts exploded about the bayou. Rene was breathing hard against me. His left arm cradled my neck.

"Lucy, you okay?" Rene pressed his lips against my forehead.

"Yes," I said.

"We're here!" Rene waved his hand toward his workers. He helped me to my feet and brushed off my dress.

"I'm not sure who the shooter's after anymore," I said.

"This stalking shit is over as of now." Rene helped me into the boat.

"What are you going to do?" I sat next to the captain's seat, wondering if the shooter was Bubba?

"Set a trap." Rene's mouth was set in grim determination.

CHAPTER NINETEEN

RACHEL BECKER WENT HOME THE next day. The doctor told her to take it easy.

"Don't forget," she reminded me on her way out the door, "I've got an exclusive when this case comes to a head."

I blew out a sigh. If only she knew the story behind the story: Leah Ellis and Jetta Angelo, to name a couple of suspects. Junior was home from the hospital, according to Mr. Mack.

I went down to the marina. Mr. Wilkes had just opened the rear doors of the dock house to help Mikey Mayo load a crate of whole catfish and three crates of fillets into his refrigerated truck. The fish was going to the Mayo Seafood Restaurant, which his parents ran.

Mikey was a cocky seventeen-year-old teenager with buckteeth and a shock of red hair. He was shorter than his brothers, only five foot seven inches, but as strong as a bull.

"How's it going, Mikey?" I asked. I felt sorry for this kid. He was the runt of the family. The Mayo brothers were known for being tall, dark, and handsome.

"So-so, Miss DelRose," he said. He shoved the last crate of catfish inside the truck, wrote out a receipt, and handed it to Mr. Wilkes.

"Haven't seen you out fishing of late," Mr. Wilkes commented.

"Too hot for any casting," Mikey said. He turned abruptly and climbed back inside the truck, slammed the door shut, and pulled out onto the gravel drive.

"Real talkative, ain't he?" Mr. Wilkes said, shaking his head.

"Can't figure out what happened to Mikey. He must be a throwback to a Mayo decedent nobody knew of." I helped Mr. Wilkes secure the rear doors.

Gran motored down the driveway on her red scooter, and Joey followed with a lunch basket.

"I'm glad to see you using your scooter again." I held the dock gate open for her.

"Mommy, Gran says she needs to keep it charged so as not to get rusted." Joey placed the lunch basket on the picnic table, and I opened the umbrella to give us shade. We all sat down and consumed our lunch.

"I can't help thinking something else is going on here besides Mrs. Junior's death," Mr. Wilkes commented.

"What do you mean, Mr. Wilkes?" Joey asked as he licked tuna fish from his fingers.

I gave Mr. Wilkes a warning glance. I had not told Joey of the shooting incident yesterday, only him and Gran.

"He means we have a grabbling event to talk about," I said, finishing my sandwich and chips.

"We gonna have lots of fried catfish to eat at the grabbling tournament?" Joey wanted to know.

"More than even you can eat, little mister." I tickled his tummy, and Joey squealed with laughter

Later that evening, Rene picked me up in his truck. We were going barhopping to set a trap for the stalker. Rene had hired a couple of security men to watch us from a distance. We started off at the Blue Bird Bar & Grill. Rene was like a bronze god among peasants as we made our way to the bar. Women stopped talking to ogle him and dream wet dreams. Men gave him a nod of respect. Rene wore tight blue jeans and a black cotton western shirt, the sleeves rolled up to his elbows. His long black hair was secured at the neck with one of my blue ribbons. My silk dress shimmered as I walked to the glass-top bar. I wore high-heeled sandals. My hair swung about my waist, capturing the glittering strobe lights. I felt like a princess.

After the bartender took our order, Rene covered my right hand with his and stroked my fingers. This was our first actual date, and yet it wasn't a date so much as a setup.

"You think the stalker is watching us now?" I took a sip of my peach schnapps, savoring the smooth fruity taste as it branched out, warming my blood all the way to my toes.

"The stalker could also be Sue Ann's killer," he said taking a sip of his Old Charter.

From the far end of the bar, Todd Baker, chairman of the Grabbling Event, came around and shook hands with Rene and wished us luck at the tournament. He was so bowlegged it was like watching him ride an invisible horse out the front door.

The band struck up a tune and Rene pulled me onto the dance floor and into his arms to a lively two-step. His body was hard under the western shirt and I forgot why we were there. I stepped to the rhythm of the music. Rene towered over me as he twirled me around and around until I was dizzy. I laughed clinging to him. Other dancers accidently bumped against us in their merriment.

Suddenly gunfire exploded around us shattering glass panels and light fixtures. The manic crowd scattered like stampeding cattle. Patrons dove under tables and behind the bar. The front entrance was bathed in a bright light of bursting gunpowder. Spent shells clattered onto the brick floor like gold coins. Screams were bouncing off me. Liquid amber ran down the walls as Rene pushed me out the back door.

The humid air soaked me through. My hands shook and I clenched them to my sides.

"Hurry," Rene said. "We need to make our way around the building and back up front. I've got to see who's doing all the shooting." He grasped my wrist, pulling me forward.

We tore through the weeds to a neglected alley leading back to the main street. When we rounded the building, the sound of gunfire had ceased and lights flashed from police cars and ambulances braked in front of the Blue Bird Bar & Grill.

"Where the hell are the security guys?" Rene said. He strode up to the door.

"Sorry, sir." One of the police officers stepped forward to block our path.

"We were inside and escaped out the back door," Rene said, extending his hand to show the officer the stamped neon print of a blue bird.

"Wait here and I'll get the captain," the officer said, and entered the bar.

"Look at all the shells." I pointed to the scattered casings in the entryway. There were so many police cars with flashing lights, I had to turn away to stop the red spots from blinding me.

"I'm Captain Martin. Can I have your name?" The captain was a large man with a girth wider than Santa Claus. His bushy mustache was the only hair upon his head. Rene gave him his name and address.

"This is Miss Lucy DelRose, my date," Rene said, squeezing my fingers. His eyes caressed my face and I felt myself blush.

I suddenly realized my nylon hose had become torn after our hike through the back alley. Dried blood from sharp edges of discarded boxes had left scratches on my legs. My hair had tangles.

"Miss DelRose, can you tell me what you witnessed here tonight?" Captain Martin asked.

"Rene and I were dancing. Suddenly I heard rapid shots being fired and glass shattered all around us. I could see the spent shells littering the floor." I held onto Rene's hand.

The captain turned toward Rene. "Mr. Caron, is this also what you saw?"

"Yes," Rene said. "The shooter was dressed all in black and firing an automatic rifle into the crowd. Was anyone hurt?"

"No one seriously hurt," said the captain. "The perpetrator aimed at the glass walls and ceilings. More of a scare tactic. Did you get any sense of male or female?"

"No. The shooter was less than six foot tall. I could tell because I'm six foot two and I have to bend down a little when I enter the front door. The shooter stood in the doorway, with a good three to four inches of space above their head." Rene pressed me against his thigh.

"Okay, this will do for now." Captain Martin said. "I'll contact you later if I need anything more." He went back inside the bar.

I was glad no one was hurt.

"Their surveillance cameras should tell us more. I'll contact Sheriff Ware." Rene pulled me along to his truck.

"Where are your security guys?" I asked, settling against the velour bucket seats.

"I'm calling them now." Rene flipped open his cell phone and tapped in the number, then pressed the speaker button.

A voice answered at the other end.

"Where the hell are you two?" Rene shouted.

"We're following the shooter, Mr. Caron," said a male voice.

"For Pete's sake, why didn't you call before now?" Rene barked at him.

"Sir, Sid and I didn't want to lose him. We're on Interstate 20 heading east about ten miles from Bunge doing about eighty miles an hour. This dude is hauling ass in a new white Chevy truck."

"Okay, hang in there. I'll notify the police. Don't get too close." Rene ordered me to stay put, then jumped out of the truck and ran back inside the bar.

A few moments later, he came out with Captain Martin. The captain gestured to two other officers and they took off in separate police cars. Then the captain spoke into a radio attached to his shoulder.

Rene came back to the truck. "The captain has an alert out to all counties from here to Hinds to stop that truck and apprehend the shooter. I'd really like to be there when they arrest this guy. Wanna come with me?"

"You bet your sweet ass," I said. I might finally meet this Bubba character the hippie, Ricky Downs, had called at Blue Bird Bar & Grill.

"Sweet ass? Why Miss DelRose, I do declare!" Rene laughed.

We swept through Bunge County and hit Interstate 20 within about fifteen minutes. Traffic was light. Rene pushed his truck to eighty-five miles per hour. I hung onto the bucket seat and prayed.

The nightlights slipped past as we left the small surrounding towns and came to open land filled with cotton bolls glowing with each passing headlight.

We had gone about thirty miles when Rene's cell phone rang. He answered and began to slow his speed as he listened to the caller.

"Chevy went off the bridge near Clinton and into a creek. The shooter ran into the woods. Police have dogs chasing him now," said the security guy.

"Okay, Brad. If the police don't need you, head back. I'll see you both at the shop." Rene disconnected.

"Oh, Rene, I wanted this to end tonight." I was wound up like a top.

"It will be all right, baby. We'll get the son-of-a-bitch. The police have the dogs after him. It'll be hard running in those woods at night." Rene crossed an emergency median and drove back home.

CHAPTER TWENTY

"**L**UCY, THE BIRDWATCHERS CLUB WILL be here first thing in the morning," Gran said. "They want to spend a few hours over in the woods across the river." She took a bite of her scrambled eggs.

"Do I pack a lunch like last time?" I arranged the bacon and eggs on my plate to make room for a glob of strawberry jam.

"Yes, honey. Remember Mrs. Blanc hates mustard on her sandwich." Gran finished her breakfast.

"Joey can come with us, if he wants." I scraped my plate.

"You can't go without a bodyguard," Gran said, pointing a finger at me. "I don't think bringing Joey is a good idea. Too many potshots been taken at you." She rubbed my back, her way of showing deep concern.

"Okay, Gran. I'll call Sayers Security Company and have Mr. Sayers assigned someone to me." Referring to the security crew we hired the last time there was trouble.

"I'll call Hunter," Gran said, referring to her attorney friend, a close friend to Mr. Sayers. "Hunter can fill Mr. Sayers in on our situation."

Later that afternoon, Suzanne Mayo of Mayo Seafood Restaurant came by to put in an order for an after-tournament party for the winners of the Grabbling Event. She went through all the fresh whole catfish and most of the fillets.

"If you catch any bass, add that to my list." Mrs. Mayo's balloon dress billowed about her plumb figure. "Mikey will be by tomorrow afternoon to pick up the order. Saturday is right around the corner. Good luck, Lucy dear. I hope your team wins." She patted my cheek.

"Thank you, Mrs. Mayo. I'll look out for Mikey," I said giving her a warm smile. She was a sweetheart.

A couple of hours later, Mr. Wilkes hosed down the dock and the outside of the dock house to cool things off. He turned on the mist fans to refresh us.

"Who's gonna protect you for the morning run across the river?" Mr. Wilkes gave me one of his penetrating looks.

"Sayers Security has a man coming first thing," I said, giving him a punch in the arm.

"Okay, but I'm really worried about the Grabbling Event. How are they going to protect you underwater?" Mr. Wilkes leaned against the dock railing. "Most times you can't see the hand in front of your face when all them bodies begin stirring up the sediment down there."

"Oh, Mr. Wilkes, if you only knew how tired I am of it all. First," I began counting off my fingers, "poor Sue Ann gets it, then Gran and I go into the river. Rene was next, and after that someone shot at me and Rene. Rachel is shot at the dear camp and then Junior and I end up in a ditch." I looked out over the river at the sun settling in the west, releasing a big sigh.

"You know, Miss Lucy, I think there are two different people out to get you for two different reasons." He turned to me.

"How you figure?" I scrunched my forehead in thought.

"Well, first time, when you were shoved into the river, they wanted you dead. Next time, the victim was Rene, not you. Rachel got shot on the island, but the true target was you. Junior kidnapped you, but the same blue truck rams Junior's truck and both of you are hurt. Yet the first time you're rammed, Junior isn't with you, so you're the target of the last one." Mr. Wilkes was counting the attacks on his fingers, too. "I think someone is mad at Rene and wants him to suffer. Sue Ann's killer is after you and Junior for getting too close to the truth."

I recited the information Rene had phoned in to me that morning. "The video from the police car did get the license tag of the white truck, but they found out it was stolen from the police pound. The attacker left an automatic rifle inside the truck, but the serial numbers had been scratched off. No fingerprints. It wasn't a match to the casing they found at the deer camp or any at the bar, but the video did pick up an image resembling a man."

A diesel engine rumbled down the gravel drive, interrupting our discussion. It was the Mayo's truck, with Mikey Mayo at the wheel.

"I'll go open the rear door while you start stacking the fish," I said. Mr. Wilkes nodded. I walked to the back door and stood on the loading dock while Mikey backed up to the ramp.

Once the truck was in position, Mikey jumped down from the cab and walked over to me. He had a new swagger that I'd never seen before. He opened the rear doors of the truck and dropped the lift gate even with our loading dock, then rolled out the dolly and started easing stacks of boxed fish into the truck. Mr. Wilkes went back into the stockroom to bring out more fish. Mickey paused, wiped the sweat from his face, and grinned at me.

"You looking real nice, Miss Lucy." He leaned closer to me with a bucktooth smile.

"Why thank you, Mikey," I mumbled, looking down at my clipboard to check off each of the loaded boxes.

Mikey flashed his toothy grin at me again. His orange hair, ugly features, and buckteeth weren't hampering this seventeen-year-old.

He accepted the receiving ticket, signed it, and handed it back to me as Mr. Wilkes rolled our dolly back into the stockroom.

"If that don't beat all," I said staring after the Mayo truck.

"What?" Mr. Wilkes dusted off his coveralls.

"Mikey just paid me a compliment."

"Miracles do happen." Mr. Wilkes proceeded to lock up the rear doors.

Early the next morning, I had the boat loaded with picnic baskets, life-jackets and drinks for the birdwatchers. They began arriving at 5:30 a.m. I loaded their gear while Mr. Wilkes helped each lady on board and then waved us off as I trimmed the prop down into the water. My security guard, Clay Lyons, settled next to me on an upturned plastic bucket. He was about five foot ten inches tall, with brown hair, and the beginnings of a beard. He wore sunglasses and a casual shirt and khakis.

"Miss DelRose, do you expect to be out in the open like this all day?" he said. Around his waist was a holster with a .38 automatic gun.

"We'll be at our landing site in about twenty minutes." I assured him.

"Lucy, dear, I believe we're going to have a lovely day," Mrs. Blanc, the president of the birdwatcher's group, said.

"I think you're right, Mrs. Blanc." I smiled at her and the other ladies. There were three older gentlemen in the group, but they were usually drowned out by the seven women.

The Mississippi River was a little rough this morning with heavy traffic. I eased the runabout into the main channel, heading southwest to Louisiana. We bucked the backwash from a tugboat laden with barges heading downriver to New Orleans. Cool breezes sprayed our faces with mist.

"Oh, look group, a hawk!" Mrs. Blanc raised her eyes to the heavens where a hawk soared. It screeched with delight. The others opened their notepads to write with miniature pencils.

Our landing site was up ahead. I trimmed the prop out of the water and we rode the wave up onto the sandbar. Clay helped me secure the boat. Mrs. Blanc wanted the group to explore for awhile, then come back to eat lunch. While they set off, Clay and I found shade under a magnolia tree. The fragrance of the huge white flowers was cloying.

Rene had not been happy when I told him I was taking the birdwatchers out today.

"Get Mr. Wilkes to take them across," Rene had argued.

"He's got a couple of fifty-pound catfish that have to be dressed by noon," I countered.

"Lucy..." he roared, but I disconnected. Rene didn't need the aggravation of arguing with me.

When the birdwatchers returned, a couple of hours later, we ate our picnic lunch. The group decided to explore for thirty more minutes.

I went behind a bush for a bathroom break while Clay stood guard a few feet away. The berry bushes tickled my backside. I pulled up my jeans, stepped back and screamed bloody murder, falling to the ground in intense pain.

Clay came running. Steel jaws dug into my ankle. My jeans took the severe damage while the tips of the teeth just broke the skin.

"Hold on, Miss DelRose," Clay said, kneeling down next to me. He took a handkerchief from his back pocket and wrapped it around his right hand, then grasped the steel jaws, seeming to need all his strength to pry the teeth apart. I pulled my leg out quickly. Only then did he release the steel jaws. They snapped shut. I shuddered, thinking about the poor animal that could have had its foot cut off.

"Do you have a first-aid kit in the boat?" Clay asked. I nodded. Clay scooped me up into his arms and carried me to the runabout.

The cuts were not deep, but they stung like hellfire from the antiseptic he applied.

"I'll wrap your ankle in light gauze to keep out dirt." He took a roll out of the kit and taped the gauze to my ankle.

As Clay finished, the birdwatchers emerged from the woods laughing and talking in comfortable companionship.

I scrambled to my feet, not wanting them to know about my injury. Clay helped me hustle them into the runabout. We headed for open water. My ankle throbbed from the teeth wounds left by the trap, but the cool air and mist from the river eased the tension running down my spine.

Clay kept a keen eye out while I eased the runabout into our slip.

An hour later, Gran applied fresh dressing to my ankle while I drank a glass of iced tea and swallowed two Tylenols.

Mr. Wilkes was shaking his head as he watched us.

"Do you ever go anywhere without something bad happening to you?"

"Come to think of it, I've had some bad luck lately." I gave him a wiry grin and a shrug.

"That is an understatement," Gran said.

"Mommy, what happened?" Joey came in from his room and noticed Gran tending my ankle.

"I stepped into a trap this morning." I hugged him to me and I nuzzled his hair. He smelled of fresh air and sunshine.

"Mommy, I'm not a baby!" Joey struggled out of my arms, but stayed by my side. He would always be my baby.

CHAPTER TWENTY-ONE

THE RINGING PHONE WOKE ME and I glanced at the clock, five o'clock. I stumble into the kitchen and I answered it. "Hello."

"Lucy, dear, I'm so sorry for disturbing you at this ungodly hour, but we need help with setting up the Grabbling Event." Cricket's unmistakably cheerful voice hummed through the wires.

"Help?" I yawned loudly, scratching my head.

"Yes, dear. I had ten people lined up to lay the dance floor, set up the cookers, and unfold the bleachers, but two of them had to go out-of-town due to a death in the family. Please say you'll give us a hand this morning. Won't need you but three hours tops," Cricket added in her most persuasive voice.

"All right, Cricket. Let me grab a bite of breakfast first," I said.

"Thanks so much. I just need one more body there. See you." She said ending the call.

I rushed through a shower, braided my hair and wolfed down eggs and toast.

"Gracious, child, where are you off to in such a hurry?" Gran bustled into the kitchen, slipping an apron over her housedress.

"Cricket called. Two helpers went AWOL and she needs help setting up the Grabbling Event this morning." I gulped my water.

"Take Mr. Wilkes with you as a body guard," Gran insisted.

"Gran, we need Mr. Wilkes here. I'll call Clay Lyons at Sayers Security." I took out my cell phone and spoke with Mr. Sayers. He arranged for Clay to meet me at the bend in the river on the bank.

Joey entered the kitchen, rubbing the sleep out of his eyes.

"Mommy, where are you going?" He noticed my purse hanging from my shoulder.

"I have to help set up the Grabbling Event for a couple of hours this morning. How about giving Gran a hand in the dock house?" I kissed his cheek, which was still warm from sleep.

"Oh, Mommy, how come I can't go?" he moaned.

"Well, I think with so many mishaps coming my way, it's best you stay close to home. How about we play a game of Nintendo tonight to make up for it?" I traded.

"I suppose. I'm going to be at the Grabbling Event tomorrow, right?" His brown eyes drowned mine.

"Yes, sweetheart, you and Gran will be there to cheer me and Mr. Wilkes," I assured him.

"Okay." He turned to his grandmother. "Gran, I'm hungry."

I waved to them as I left through the garage door and jumped into our Chevy truck. We still had not replaced the station wagon.

A short while later, I drove up to the event site. Cricket had everyone working. Clay met me as I walked up to the others.

"Cricket put me to work the minute I set foot on the ground," he said with a laugh.

"That's our Cricket," I said.

Cricket and the rest of the volunteers laughed and threw playful insults at each other while setting up the equipment. The cookers were left to the men. Clay and I unfolded the bleachers and arranged them around the dance floor, helped hang lanterns on nearby trees for nightlight. The river breezes kept the mosquitoes at bay and the sun hid behind the clouds, seeming to take pity on our hard work. I hoped it did not rain tomorrow. It would spoil everything.

Clay and I walked back to the truck to pull out a cooler I kept there for emergencies. I took out two cold Cokes, throwing one to Clay. He appeared to be keeping cool wearing a white muscle shirt and casual cotton shorts. His .38 was holstered about his waist. Cricket hadn't been able to keep her eyes off him all morning.

"Hey, you two, we've got treats to eat," she called out.

"Be right there." I knew she wanted to talk with Clay.

Clay followed me closely. To the casual observer we appeared to be a couple.

"Coming to the event tomorrow?" Cricket asked him.

Clay looked at me and I nodded. "I'll be here," he said.

"Good. I need an extra cook." She pinned a grin my way and I laughed. Cricket was a scamp.

"Cricket, Clay is my body guard," I confided in her. "Keep a low profile on this."

"I'm sorry, Lucy. I didn't know. Of course, he needs to be close to you in the water." Cricket blush a soft red.

"He'll probably be in the boat, but once we're on land, we'll both give you a hand." I patted her arm.

I made my way down toward the river's edge and looked out over the catfish site. Clay stood next to me.

"How far will you swim out?" He gestured at the water.

"We go in from the boats. The barrels are scattered in a circle about fifty feet out."

The wind picked up and I lifted my face to feel it. The smell of river water and cedar trees made me glad to be alive. Clay stood in front of me.

"Let's not give someone an easy target," he said.

"You're right. Okay, let's head in," I tossed my empty Coke can in the trash and Clay did the same. We waved to Cricket.

"See you tomorrow," I called out to her. "Clay, I'll meet you at the marina tomorrow morning at eight." He nodded. We climbed into our vehicles and headed out.

I powered down my windows to let in fresh air. I'd started to press the button to roll them up when I saw a brown and black spotted puppy caught in fish netting along the waterfront. The poor thing was strangling itself trying to escape. I quickly pulled over next to the river's edge and hopped out of the truck. The puppy wagged his tail when he saw me. I knelt down and felt his wet fur and quivering body. He licked my hand, whimpering his pain. I gently removed the netting, noticing blood oozing from cuts the net had made pressing against his skin. When I pulled the last of the netting that bound his feet, he gave me wet *thank you* kisses. I laughed to see his happiness at gaining freedom.

With a sudden whoosh and a strong gust of air, something heavy sailed past my head and struck the cottonwood tree next to me. An arrow was embedded in its trunk. A second arrow could be heard heading my way. I released the puppy and dove for the ground. The clouds blocked out the sun and blanketed the woods in darkness. I scampered behind a clump of bushes, trying to make out the bowman. The puppy found me and licked my hand in continued gratitude. I appreciated his tenderness, but he had revealed my location.

I scooped up the puppy and headed deeper into the woods, loosing myself. The bowman followed. Arrows kept whooshing as they left his bow, striking trees right and left. Finally it occurred to me that he was deliberately missing his mark, enjoying the chase. I stopped running and slipped the puppy inside my shirt, then I scrunched down next to an old wrecked aluminum boat and waited. The bowman passed me in the darkness of the trees under the overcast sky. Suddenly the clouds parted, lighting up the woods and the man standing with his back to me. The puppy yelped, eager to be noticed. The bowman turned to me with his bow at ready. I screamed, fell backward against the boat I'd been using for cover. Then a figure flew through the air and tackled the bowman. The wooden bow and arrow fell to the ground. The tussle was violent, with hard hitting knuckles against bone. In the blur of bodies, I realized one was Clay with his white muscle shirt and cotton shorts. The other man was covered in black sports gear that included a face mask. The bowman was short, but muscular. He sucker punched Clay in the groin, then darted away, sprinting deeper into the woods leaving Clay in agony. In his hast, the bowman forgot his equipment.

"You okay?" I knelt down next to Clay. "Want me to get you some ice?"

"No!" Clay exploded, then settled back down. His breathing was shallow and it took a while before he was able to stand up.

"Why did you leave yourself open like that?" Clay accused me.

"The puppy was in pain. I didn't think." The puppy thanked me again by licking my face.

"Miss DelRose, I can't protect you if you refuse to ignore the dangers around you," Clay said as we made our way through the woods back to the vehicles. I had retrieved the bow and arrow. They were heavy.

"I know and I'm sorry. But I get so tired of looking over my shoulder." I complained. "It's like being a public figure. I don't know how celebrities do it?"

"They respect their body guards," Clay came back at me. I frowned.

"I'll need to drop off this puppy at the vet's for treatment," I said. I got into my truck.

"I'll follow you. Please drive slow. My reflexes are a bit numb right now."

And so it went until I pulled into the marina an hour later. Mr. Wilkes had dressed the fish for the afternoon customers. Joey and Gran were up in the house preparing lunch. I told Mr. Wilkes what had happened.

"Where's the bow and arrow?" Mr. Wilkes said.

"They're in the truck. I'm calling the sheriff to have it dusted for fingerprints. I didn't want to keep touching it." I flipped open my cell phone and made the call.

The sheriff said he'd send Deputy Griggs to pick up the evidence and he would also talk with Clay about the bowman.

"Miss Lucy, you handled that very well," Mr. Wilkes said proudly.

"Thank you. Let's go have lunch. I'm starved."

CHAPTER TWENTY-TWO

I ADJUSTED THE RED BANDANA over my hair and slipped into the waters of the Mississippi River in search of the rusted barrel. Silt of bygone days danced before me over river grass and algae. My heartbeat pounded in my ears while I held my breath. Old tires lay half buried in mud, a hideout for smaller marine life. Lazy schools of striped bass moved alongside me brushing my shirt-sleeve on their way downriver. A swamp moccasin darted after the bass, and they scattered in self-preservation. I looked up through the rippling current, which trapped the afternoon sun and bathed my underwater world in splashes of red and brown tones.

Mr. Wilkes joined me beneath the water carrying a short length of pipe.

I stepped forward into the muck of riverbed soil and spied the barrel wedged under an eroding bank. I cautiously approached the creature's dwelling. Swallowing a lump of air at the base of my throat, I grabbed the open end of the barrel and shoved my gloved hand inside the black abyss. The barrel shook when the creature tried to elude me. Dirt billowed about me. Mr. Wilkes banged the side of the barrel with the pipe to scare the hell out of its resident. In one whoosh, the creature lunged out of the barrel and latched himself onto my hand, digging sharp teeth into my glove. I pulled the big flat-head catfish out of his lair, wrestling him as he whacked me with his tail in a desperate attempt at freedom. His sleek skin rubbed against my bare forearm, his body writhing to and fro, while I held fast to the roof of his mouth. I tried to keep my balance as I pushed hard against the riverbed toward the surface, breaking free, and gulping fresh air. I cradled the flat-head catfish under my arm and held him like a kid you'd try to hustle out of the toy store.

The catfish announced he was tired of my manhandling by biting harder on my gloved hand and I yelped in pain. His forty-odd pounds were a burden to bear against my slight frame. I pressed him tighter against my side. Mr. Wilkes broke surface beside me and supported my grip on the catfish while we headed toward the bank amid the applause of the spectators who'd come out for the annual Grabbling Event.

Gran and Joey came over and hugged me. Rachel Becker approached with her camera crew. Todd Baker, the chairman of the Grabbling Event, took possession of our catfish. It weighed in at forty-nine pounds, six ounces. I cheered. We were in the lead. Four other teams had gone ahead of us. It would be Rene and Royce in the water now.

Rene, dressed in cut-offs and a dark muscle shirt, flipped over backwards from a small runabout into the river. Royce followed.

Gran handed me a towel and I dried off, never taking my eyes off the rippling water where Rene had disappeared. The crowd seemed to hold their breath, waiting for the last team to surface. The water level near the bank grew higher and higher as a fight pursued underwater. I started to run toward the river, but Mr. Wilkes held me back.

"He has Royce down there. They'll be all right," Mr. Wilkes said.

I nodded, but couldn't stop trembling. Thrashing, white foam bubbled about as Rene surfaced fighting a monster. I gripped Mr. Wilkes's arm in panic. Rene's right arm was clamped between razor teeth and a long snout. The monster's body was at least ten feet long, and looked like it weighed over 300 pounds. Good Lord, it was an alligator gar! The huge gray-scaled body was equipment with razor teeth and the appearance of a menacing alligator. It looked at Rene with little black beady eyes. Royce was trying to pry open its mouth to release Rene's arm. Several men jumped into the water to fight the fight all fishermen find themselves in from time to time. The river held untold creatures of prehistoric stature. Five men held the alligator gar in a death grip as they walked him out of the river.

Todd Baker approached Rene, stopped, and looked down at the gar.

"Rene, you're team provided us with the most entertainment today, but I'm sorry to say this creature is not a catfish," he said. The crowd laughed.

"Todd, it doesn't matter. I lost to a beautiful woman. What more could a man ask for?" Rene said, sweeping his arm in my direction. Blood dripped from the teeth marks. Cricket came running with a first-aid kit and tended to his wounds. Rene's wet hair was tangled about his broad shoulders and Cricket had difficulty keeping her eyes on his wounds.

"Rene, I'll get you a towel," I volunteered. Anything to get away from his disturbing eyes. I approached the camper trailer where Cricket had stored supplies for the teams and was reaching in to grab a towel when someone grabbed me from behind. For a split second I thought it was Clay about to scold me for walking off without him, but no. The fingernails belonged to a woman. Jetta Angelo snatched a handful of my wet hair and yanked it so hard the pain brought tears to my eyes. I fell back against her, accidently knocking her onto the grassy bank. Winded, I lay on top of her for a couple of seconds before Jetta crunched my neck in the crock of her arm. Gasping for air, I elbowed her ribs. She let out a shriek, rolled over, and pinned me beneath her. I wrapped her black hair around my wrist and jerked with all the strength I could muster.

Her screech brought the crowd, eager to watch two women in a catfight. We had one another's head, pulling hair, and thumping skulls against the ground. I rammed my knee into her groin. She snarled like an animal and went for my throat. But Junior Dykes shoved her backwards and she landed on her ass.

The crowd groaned in disapproval. They'd enjoyed the entertainment. Rene appeared above me as I lay on the grass recovering from my ordeal. My head ached to the roots from Jetta's manhandling. Junior pushed his way ahead of Rene, held out his hand to help me up. I took it and managed to get to my feet. Joey ran over to me.

"Mommy, are you okay?" He wrapped his arms around my waist, burying his face against my stomach.

"Yes, I think so, sweetheart." I stroked his hair, watching as Rene grabbed Jetta by the arm, yanking her to her feet, and dragged her away from the camper and out of my sight. I sighed.

"Lucy, let me help you." Gran put her arm around my waist and led me to our truck. She helped me change into dry clothes so that we could enjoy eating the catfish we caught.

The fire under the cookers fried the fish to perfection. Mr. Wilkes piled his plate full and handed it off to his ladylove, Rita. Rita was Creole and half African American. Her dark eyes slanted upward giving her an oriental look. Her cheekbones were pronounced, and her red lips were provocative. No wonder Mr. Wilkes fell in love with her. All their children and grandchildren were here to cheer for my partner. With his help, we had won this year's Grabbling Event.

During the trophy award, which was presented after dinner, Junior appeared at my side, sexy in tight jeans and a dark blue T-shirt. His wavy dark hair fell forward across his eyes when he looked down at me. Junior made me nervous, and I edged toward Mr. Wilkes. Sheriff Ware had wanted to charge Junior with kidnapping the other night when he forced me into his truck. I was hesitant to charge a friend who I knew was suffering from a guilty conscious.

"Well, Lucy, I hope you're not the worse for wear after your wrestling match," Cricket joked. The crowd roared with laughter and clapped. The men gave me a wolf whistle.

"I'm fine, Cricket," I acknowledged their playfulness.

"Lucy DelRose and her partner Mr. William Wilkes are this year's winner in our annual Grabbling Event." Cricket handed each of us a gold-plated trophy with a catfish mounted on top and I was given a check in the amount of Ten Thousand Dollars, a contribution from our sponsors.

"I want to thank my family for supporting me. I especially wish to thank my partner, Mr. Wilkes." I hugged him.

Joey was jumping up and down for attention so I gave him my trophy to hold. Mr. Wilkes handed his off to his youngest son, Billy.

"Now, we wish to award Rene Caron with a special trophy for bringing in the most unusual fish," Cricket said, tongue in cheek. She turned her back for a minute and then whipped out a stuffed toy alligator to the spectators' applause. Rene took the attention in stride, accepted the toy alligator, and gave a bow to his audience. He turned around and tossed the alligator to me. Instinctively I reached out and caught it.

"Now," Cricket yelled out. "Let's eat some dessert!" Everyone formed a line next to the cakes and pies. Cricket snagged Clay, who had been keeping himself in the background. He looked at me helplessly.

"It's all right, Clay, I've got her back." Rene slipped his arm around my waist. For a minute I thought Junior would intervene, but then he gave Rene a lopsided grin and fell in behind us. Joey and Gran piled their plates with goodies. Music surrounded us as the sun dropped to the west and the lanterns lit up the night.

An hour later, Rene pulled me onto the dance floor, hugging me tight against him. His arm was bandaged from the gar's teeth marks.

"Doesn't hurt," he murmured into my ear.

"I thought you were drowning," I whispered, my lips caressing his ear. He sucked in a breath.

"I'm drowning in you." He seduced me with his voice. My knees weakened.

His hand slipped under my T-shirt. Suddenly Junior loomed up behind Rene and tapped his shoulder to cut in.

"Junior, she's with me," Rene whirled me away to the far side of the dance floor. But Junior was not to be swayed. He stalked Rene and tapped his shoulder again.

Rene made a fist and turned to use it, but Gran suddenly appeared next to Junior.

"Lucy dear, it's time to go. I'm dead tired." She leaned on Junior. Joey joined us on the dance floor with my trophy clutched against his chest.

"Mommy, can Billy spend the night?" Joey said, looking up at me. Mr. Wilkes and his youngest son, Billy, walked over to us.

"Sure, if it's okay with you, Mr. Wilkes," I said, glad of the interruption. Rene's fist unclenched, Junior faded into the night.

"Ask your mother, Billy," Mr. Wilkes told his son. Billy ran off toward the bleachers.

Rene walked us to the truck and made sure we had all of our gear. Billy climbed in with Joey as Rene helped Gran inside.

"Thank you," I said. Rene took me by surprise and kissed me upon my lips in front of the spectators.

"I'm sorry about Jetta," he whispered next to my ear. "I want you so much, I ache inside." He pulled one of my braids.

I leaned against him unable to speak.

"Go on, get your grandmother home," he said, slipping a hand under my buttocks and lifting me into the truck. "I'll follow you back to your house." He turned and went to his truck.

I drove home like a lovesick fool.

CHAPTER TWENTY-THREE

I STRUGGLED AGAINST BINDINGS THAT held me. I couldn't open my eyes. Blindfolded! I felt the dirt floor beneath me and inhaled its earthy essence. My legs were bound at my ankles and my wrists were twisted behind my back. The air was clogged with the smells of insecticide and used oil. I was on a farm. Pushing myself into a sitting position, I scooted about the dirt floor, but didn't come in contact with a door or wall. This place must be a barn, but I didn't smell any hay, alfalfa, or manure. That meant there were no horses or cows inside. I strained to listen for noises of traffic, but found my prison to be quiet and dusty. I sneezed into my gag and tasted dirt. Ugh!

I shook my head to clear the cobwebs. What was the last thing I remembered? The Grabbling Event! No, that wasn't the last thing. I had put Joey and Billy to bed then Gran and I stayed up late to watch a movie. Gran had gone on to bed first while I went around securing windows and doors before keying in the security code. That was it! I remembered reaching out my hand to enter the code — and then everything went blank. Anger began to swell inside me. This was the last time he'd get the drop on me. This Bubba must be a man of many talents.

For Junior's sake, I hoped *he* wasn't behind my present predicament. After this stunt, my ladylike manners would be replaced with good old revenge.

I lay down upon the floor and rubbed my face against the dirt until I finally managed to work off the blindfold. I blinked a few times and saw that a new day had come without my being aware of it. I must have been unconscious since last night. Looking around, I saw tall white barrels of insecticides, and pallets filled with hoses. The barn door was closed, and the shuttered windows prevented me from seeing outside. I had no way of telling whose farm I was on. I spotted a saw-blade on a wooden table and scooted my way over to it. I stood up, hopped to the table, and turned my back to the blade. As I turned, I caught sight of a vice-grip fastened at the end of the table. I fumbled with the saw-blade until I was able to slip its handle inside the vice-grip and awkwardly turn the knob to tighten the blade. When the blade was finally tight enough, I stood on tiptoes and laid my hands on either side of the blade, gently moving them back and forth to cut the rope that bound me. By the time the rope gave way, I was exhausted. I fell upon my knees, resting, then I tore at the ropes binding my ankles. When I stood at last, I was weak and hungry. I had to get out of here before my captor came back.

I pushed against the barn door, but it was bolted from the outside. Then I tried one of the shutters, it was loose! I yanked the shutter from its hinges, scrambled out the window, and fell to the ground. By now the sun was at half-mast and the crickets sang among the endless fields of cotton bolls. I got to my feet and stumbled along the moist rows, falling in my haste to put distance between myself and the barn. Breaking free of the field, I stepped onto a black tar road and continued on.

The sun had set behind the trees when headlights suddenly beamed in my direction. Frantic, I ducked behind a cotton bush. The car didn't slow down, disappearing from sight around the curve. I sighed. If only I had my cell phone.

Just then I felt a vibration in my front pocket. I cursed in frustration. I'd had my cell phone the whole time. Why hadn't anyone tried to call me before? I dug it out of my pocket and looked at the screen.

"Hello." My voice was shaky.

"Lucy?" Rene answered doubtfully, uncertain of the caller's identity.

"Rene," I said with a sigh.

"Oh, honey." The raw emotion in his voice brought me up short.

"I'm fine, just pissed off," I reassured him.

"Where are you?" he said.

"I don't know. I woke up in a barn all tied up. I worked myself free and escaped through the middle of a cotton field going west. Then I found a tar road running north and south. A car passed, but I was afraid to stop it."

"The sheriff and I are tracking your cell phone signal. Do you see any trees in the distance? Maybe houses?" Rene urged. The warmth in his voice eased my anxiety.

"No, it's too dark now. The barn I was in didn't look familiar. There were no trees as far as I could tell when I started out." I sat down on the edge of the road.

"From the phone towers, it appears you are in the next county over." Rene sounded concerned.

"They didn't hurt Joey or Gran?" I shook with anger at the possibility.

"No, honey. Everything's okay at Rosebud. We've been looking for you since last night."

Another set of vehicle lights lit up the night illuminating the cotton field in a ghostly glow. I hurried and slid out of sight.

"A truck just passed me," I whispered into the cell phone.

"Lucy, that must have been us," Rene said, excitement in his voice.

I heard the squeal of brakes and then red backup lights came on as the truck slowly reversed toward me.

"Do you see my truck?" Rene barked.

I stood up and walked out onto the road. The truck stopped and Rene bolted from the front seat. Sheriff Ware joined him on the pavement. Rene enveloped me in his arms and I clung to him. He smelled heavenly.

"Miss DelRose, are you all right?" the sheriff asked.

"Yes," my voice was muffled against Rene's cotton shirt as I rubbed my cheek against the soft material.

"Come on, let's get you home," Rene scooped me up in his arms amid my protests.

Bouncing around on the bench seat with each pothole, I held onto the dash to keep from hitting my head on the roof, mulling over the last few days.

"What good is having security if I always get kidnapped?" I fumed.

"You need lights attached to motion sensors along your property," Sheriff Ware said. "Then the security guards would have some forewarning."

"Sounds like a good idea," Rene said.

"How long did it take Wilson to know I was gone?" I asked. Wilson was the security guard in the dock house.

"He knew right away, but by the time he got to the house, you were gone," Rene said as we hit Bunge county line.

"When y'all rewound the videotape, what did you find?" I hung onto Rene as he made a sharp turn in the road.

"He was medium height, wearing dark clothing with a hoodie to cover his head and face," Sheriff Ware recited as if reading from his notebook. "He threw you over his shoulder like a sack of potatoes, then went around to the front of the house; and out to the main road. There was a dark full-size Ford truck parked on the side of the road near the casino entrance. He dumped you in the passenger seat and then took off heading south."

"No license plate number?" I asked.

"Too far away and too dark," the sheriff replied.

"First thing in the morning, I'm having motion sensor lights installed," I said.

Rene pulled into our driveway. Gran and Joey were waiting for me in the garage.

"Mommy," Joey threw his arms around my waist and hugged me tight. I clung to him, dropping my head to meet his.

"I'm okay, sweetheart. Mommy's fine," I said and kissed his wet cheek.

"I thought you were gone forever." He gulped back a sob.

"Hey, you know you can't get rid of me." I stooped down and wrapped myself around him.

"You were kidnapped?" His voice was full of wonder.

"Yes. It was really kind of an adventure, not a scary one, but like Indiana Jones." I mentioned his favorite fictional hero, and that did it. Joey became more intrigued than scared by my time in the barn.

Gran's hand settled on my shoulder. I patted her fingers and squeezed them tightly.

Rene stayed for a while longer, until I had showered and changed into clean clothes.

The sheriff left a female deputy in charge of our safety. I wanted to chuckle. She was slight of build and came to just under my chin. Dad always said dynamite comes in small packages. If so, she should cause quite a bang.

CHAPTER TWENTY-FOUR

DEPUTY LOU ANN JONES STRADDLED a chair in the dining room as she brought me up to date on my day in the barn. The sunlight graced her honey brown skin to a healthy glow. Chocolate eyes looked into mine and there was trust between us.

"Jack Jarvis owns the barn where you were held and most of the land around it. We interviewed him this morning. He's an elderly man confined to a wheelchair after a stroke he had a few months ago. He didn't know who you were and neither did his farmhands." Deputy Jones closed her notepad.

"This all sounds a bit crazy," I said in frustration. "Why would an old man have anything to do with me or Junior Dykes?" We seemed to be taking two steps back for every one forward.

Deputy Jones shrugged her shoulders.

A few minutes later, Mr. Wilkes came in through the back kitchen door.

"Good to see you, Miss Lucy." He sat down next to me.

"It's good to see you, Mr. Wilkes." I patted his leathery brown hand.

"The workers are putting up the motion lights. This place will look like Las Vegas at night." Mr. Wilkes shook his head.

"I know, but what else can I do? Everyone keeps popping in and stealing me," I wanted to find humor in my situation, but I knew things could turn deadly.

"Well, no one's going to steal you on my watch," Deputy Jones nodded to me.

"Let's get down to the dock. We have fish to clean," I said and scooted back my chair.

Just then, Gran and Joey came into the kitchen, yawning and rubbing their eyes.

"Mommy, where are you going?" my sleepy son demanded.

"I'll be at the dock house. Eat breakfast and then you can join me." I tousled his hair and kissed his warm cheek.

"We'll both be down in about thirty minutes," Gran said. "Joey, you can begin helping with the pots and pans."

We spent the whole morning cleaning catfish and cutting up buffalo steaks.

Joey's Cub Scout den leader, Martin Keys, stopped by to let me know there would be a camp-out across the river on a sandbar tomorrow night. An older parent with two school-age boys, Martin was very tall, with salt and pepper hair.

"Miss DelRose, I'm happy to hear Joey will be able to make the camp-out. He didn't sound too sure the other day." Martin knelt down on his haunches so that I could talk to him while I sat at the table cleaning fish.

"I'll be there to give the scouts a hand," I assured him. With a lunatic on the loose, I didn't want Joey going anywhere without me.

"That's great," he said. "The scout leaders were wondering if we could use your boat to get across the river."

"No problem. We'll be happy to take everyone over," I said. I hoped the smaller boat Rene had loaned me would be large enough.

"The boys will be here about seven o'clock tomorrow evening. See you then." Martin shook Mr. Wilkes hand and smiled at the deputy and me, then walked to the dock gate.

Martin was a good den leader. Joey would be a wolf this year, since he was going into second grade.

"I better get my camping gear ready," Mr. Wilkes commented. "Billy should come along to help the boys out."

I nodded. Billy was a Boy Scout, too, and usually helped the younger ones adjust to roughing it.

"I guess this means I'll be joining you two tomorrow night?" Deputy Jones tilted her head toward me.

"Only if the sheriff orders it. I'll certainly have enough adult chaperones there." I washed off the cleaning table before wheeling the metal cart inside the dock house. Opening the refrigerator, I began storing all the fresh meat inside while Joey helped to clean the dock house.

Gran rolled down from the house on her red scooter bearing a picnic basket filled with fish sandwiches and peanut butter cookies. She offered a cookie to the deputy first.

"Mrs. DelRose, you're the only other person that makes cookies like my granny," Deputy Jones said licking her fingers.

"Why thank you, Lou Ann." Gran blushed. She made friends fast.

"Lou Ann, are you coming camping with us?" my sweet boy asked.

"Do you want me to come?" Deputy Jones's eyes melted like liquid gold.

"You bet." Joey jumped up and down.

"I'll bring my camping gear in the morning. I best bring my rod and reel and my tackle box, too. I'd love to cook some fish over an open fire." Deputy Jones motions with her hands as she pretended to cast her fishing line out into the river.

Later that evening, I was relaxing on the back porch, watching the motion sensor lights. They came on every time a car drove along the casino driveway. It was like being at a ballpark at night. No one could sneak onto our property now without being seen. Wilson was comfortably enjoying his night at the dock house knowing he was now in full control of the security.

My cell phone vibrated against my skin.

"Hello, sweetheart," Rene's voice licked its way down my body. Goosebumps began surfacing.

"Hi, yourself." My thighs tightened.

"You alone?" His voice became hoarse.

"I'm sitting in the porch swing sunbathing under the motion lights." My foot kept the swing in motion as I laid my head against the cushions and lost myself in visions of Rene's muscular physique.

"I want to make love to you," he said, his voice like a soft caress.

The goose bumps came back with a vengeance. I went limp.

"I don't know if I'm ready for you," I whispered.

"You're ready, little mermaid. I lie in my bed at night and watch my golden-hair mermaid in my fish tank and I think of you."

I remembered sleeping in his bedroom a few months back and watching his exotic fish swim in and out of sunken ships and dark caves. I thrilled at the thick cotton sheets and king-size bed. I had been with Joey, hiding out from bad guys. Rene had given up the bed for us, but his presence had remained to haunt me.

"I'm going to slip into your bed tonight when you are sleeping," he threatened me softly.

"Not unless you want Deputy Jones to shoot you," I retorted smugly.

"That would only happen if the deputy was lying next to you in bed," he chuckled.

"You're a very bad man," I scolded him.

"I know. Goodnight, little mermaid." He disconnected.

The man was good at foreplay.

CHAPTER TWENTY-FIVE

JUNIOR DYKES SHOWED UP ON the dock with his three sons at six forty-five the following evening. Mr. Wilkes mumbled something into Deputy Jones's ear, and she took a possessive step in my direction.

"Lucy, I brought the boys for the Cub Scout camp trip," Junior said matter-of-factly, ignoring Mr. Wilkes and the deputy. His dark good looks and muscular body had me wishing things had been different between him and Sue Ann. He gave the appearance of the Junior I knew long ago, before his extra-marital indiscretions.

"The boys should have a good time." I moved toward Junior's children, but Joey and Billy beat me to it.

"Gosh, David, I'm glad you could make it," Joey said, clasping the oldest brother around the shoulders.

Then Martin, the den leader, arrived and we began loading the small runabout with sleeping bags and tents.

"I'll make two runs. The first to take over the supplies and the second to come back for the boys," I said, while stepping into the boat and made room for Deputy Jones to sit on the bench seat next to me. I had made arrangements yesterday for Clay Lyons to stay with Gran while we were across the river. She wasn't happy, but she agreed.

The river traffic was light and we sped across the main channel in record time. Deputy Jones helped unload the boat of camping equipment. I popped open two cans of Coke for us and we relaxed for a couple of minutes under an oak tree that gave off plenty of shade in the late evening heat. I wore jean cutoffs and a white T-shirt to stay cool.

"I like this detail," Deputy Jones said, wiping her lips with the back of her hand. "It beats riding around in a patrol car all day." Her eyes were glowing with adventure. She wore brown uniform shorts and a matching shirt.

"Just wait until all those boys get over here and you'll be praying for a quiet car ride," I said with a laugh. "Camp fires and shenanigans from a group of Wolf Cub Scouts can take the wind out of us adults."

"Can't be any worse than a houseful of relatives day and night. I sometimes wish my momma would kick some of them out," she said, tossing her can into a trash bag.

On the trip back to the marina, I enjoyed the sudden cool breeze emanating from a tugboat and its backwash. We rocked through the aftermath with style. As we approached the dock, I could see Joey jumping up and down waving at us. I raised my hand and waved back. Joey was happy with his friends.

Mr. Wilkes helped seat each boy along the benches, their backs against the console to brace them from sudden surges of rough water. The adults hugged the front deck and side railings to balance themselves. I gave Gran a hug and kiss before jumping back into the boat. Clay met my eyes and nodded his assurance that Gran would be okay. Junior waved his farewell as he walked back to his truck.

"Watch out for snakes," Gran called out after us.

"I will, Gran," I assured her.

Just as we pulled away, Mr. Mack, Junior's dad, came to stand next to Gran. His arm dropped around her shoulders. Mr. Mack was a widower, and he and Gran had been keeping each other company for some time now. It wouldn't surprise me if they decided to marry. Gran was very strict on the moral code of marriage over fornication.

The runabout sank deeper into the river from the extra weight. I kept a steady course, avoiding the other boaters so we wouldn't have to ride out any backwash. We were only a few feet from the sandbar when a jet boat motored from the north, heading toward us with a vengeance. I throttled up, throwing us backward, and narrowly missed being broadsided by the jet boat's crazy pilot.

We helped the boys out of the boat and they splashed through an inch of water to reach the sandbar. I was breathing a sigh of relief over our narrow escape. Once everything was unloaded, I reversed the runabout back into the river. I needed room to gun the boat onto the sandbar so I could secure it for the night.

Then the jet boat was back. This time the pilot roared past and side-swiped my outboard motor. That was it! Working on adrenaline, I trimmed the prop down into the water, and against the screaming advice of everyone on the sandbar, took off after the son-of-a-bitch who didn't care a damn about hurting children.

The runabout flew over the whitecaps, banging the hull until my teeth rattled. The jet boat was a sleek red missile with silver trim sparkling in the setting sun, the pilot hunched down into the captain's chair. He must be giving the .125 horsepower motor all it had because I was gaining. My runabout was small, but the .150 horsepower motor gave her an extra kick. I threw the throttle wide open and pulled up alongside the pilot. I got a quick look at the boat's registration number. The whitecaps slammed against the hull, suddenly propelling the runabout into the jet boat, scraping her portside. Then without warning, the *Miss Queen* appeared next to us, blowing her horn long and loud as she attempted to make the wide right turn at Turtle Island. I grasped the throttle and lessened my speed, cutting the wheel sharply starboard to avoid the *Miss Queen,* and ran up onto Turtle Island, taking a few small trees with me as the boat became hung up in kudzu. Looking over my shoulder, I observed the jet boat as it hung back and took the savage beating of *Miss Queen's* backwash. But the pilot made his escape around the bend in the river, near where the catfish tournament had been held.

Damn, damn, damn. I'd never get a break in capturing this creep.

Another horn blared close by and Rene's cabin cruiser pulled up next to Turtle Island. He swung his legs over the rail, dropped into the river, and swam to the bank, splashing out of the water; his bronzed skin gleamed golden against the setting sun.

"Will you ever stop taking chances? Good God, Lucy, you nearly got yourself killed." Rene pulled me roughly from the runabout and set me before him.

"Dammit, don't you dare talk to me like a child. That creep crashed into my boat with all the Cub Scouts right there waiting to set up for night camp. I'm not an imbecile, thank you very much. I've managed to live twenty-nine years without getting killed and I expect I'll get through another twenty-nine without you screaming at me. I'm going to catch that bastard and no one's going to stop me, including you," I yelled up at him. The sun was in my eyes, and I couldn't read to see how he was taking my independent talk. Then he gripped my arms and lifted me up where I could see him, blocking out the sun. Rene's jaw was clenched tight, his eyes like black coals.

"I've never wanted to slap a woman like I want to slap you right now," he breathed heavily, bruising my arms with his fingers.

"Go ahead if it'll make you feel better," I said, my voice dropping to deathly calm. I was tired of all the pampering. It wasn't getting us anywhere. My life was being run by everyone except me.

Still holding me up against his chest, Rene grabbed the back of my head and forced my mouth against his, punishing me with his lips. But the kiss turned tender as he wrapped his arms around me.

"You're such a brat," he said against my lips before dropping me to my feet. I immediately missed the warmth and security I felt within his arms.

"Let's haul the runabout back into the water," he said and swam back to his boat to unwind the winch. We spent the next hour slowing dragging the runabout out of the kudzu and into the river. Rene checked the damaged motor and controls to see if the boat would get me back upriver.

All I could think about was getting my revenge on that son-of-a-bitch and his red jet boat.

CHAPTER TWENTY-SIX

"WHAT DOES THIS MEAN?" I said, slapping a document on the desk in front of Rene. We were in his office at the welding shop. Earlier that morning, I had asked Sheriff Ware to run the registration numbers of the red jet boat. He had one of his deputies fax me a copy of the form from the Department of Wildlife, Parks, & Fisheries. Rene Caron's name was listed as the registered owner.

"It means that I once owned this boat years ago," Rene said, calmly examining the registration document. He had tied his black hair back with one of my blue ribbons.

"*It means* that you recognized the boat and said nothing," I said through clenched teeth. My toes curled within my sneakers, I was so pissed.

"I've owned hundreds of boats over the years. I buy and sell used boats as well as build new ones. I'm surprised the owner didn't register the boat in his name after we signed the papers. But I remember this boat." He fingered the document again, his skin glossy with sweat. "It was sold to a Harvey James last fall."

"Rene, I will not be lied to. Either you're forthright with me, or our friendship is over." I turned my back on him. Tears sprang to my eyes, but I held firm as I walked out of the office toward the back door of the welding shop. Like a panther he came after me, sliding his arms around my waist and drawing me back against his hard body.

"I'm always honest with you, Lucy," he said, and then pressed his lips against the side of my neck.

"What can I think, after you remained silent?" I whispered, but relaxed against his form.

"I had to be sure Mr. James still owned the boat. I found out earlier this morning that he passed away four months ago and the executor of his estate sold all his property. He's supposed to call me back with the name of the new owner. This time, I'm going to make sure my name is taken off of the boat's registration." He rubbed his hands up and down my arms, soothing my nerves.

"If it was only my safety I had to worry about yesterday, I wouldn't have come here today," I told him. "But I was responsible for the Cub Scout troop. I can't afford to be lax in my judgment of people."

Rene's hands slowly stroked my skin. My breath quickened. The heat of his body soaked the back of my T-shirt and I began to tremble.

"I am your most loyal subject, and we're much more than just friends." Rene turned me around and looked into my eyes. His irises darkened. I met his lips halfway, enjoying the kiss. Wolf whistles broke us apart as Rene's crew clapped their hands with enthusiasm. Rene turned toward them and bowed at the waist. My cheeks turning red, I escaped through the back door.

"Hey!" Rene called after me.

"Yes?" I said turning around, breathless.

"I'll have your boat ready tonight. I'll see you in the morning." He blew me a kiss and went back to work.

Whew! What an afternoon.

Later that evening after Mr. Wilkes went home to Rita, Gran and I sat at the picnic table and watched the sun dissolve into the river, shimmering with the colors of the rainbow. Clay and Deputy Jones stood over at the dock rail, talking.

"Can you trust, Rene?" Gran asked after I told her about the jet boat.

"I can't think of a reason not to," I said, still focused on appreciating the colors swimming before my eyes.

"This thing with Rene — is it serious?" she asked, taking my hand into hers.

"Gran, my heart says yes, but my head's putting up a fight," I said with a laugh and I released my hair from its scrunchie, shaking the stands free to blow gently in the evening breeze.

"Lucy, honey, has Rene asked you to marry him?" Gran stroked my hair.

"Well, it was more like he *told* me than asked me," I admitted.

"How do you feel about that?"

"I feel like I'm losing control of my life," I answered.

"You mean you're nervous about trusting another man?" Gran knew about the disaster of my first marriage. It had been fraught with abuse and betrayal.

"Yes, that is a big concern." I shook my hair back from my face.

"Don't be afraid to give your heart. If Rene truly loves you and Joey, he won't control you; he'll embrace your talents and ambitions." Gran grasped both my hands in hers.

"Let's wait and see what happens. Right now, we have to find the person who is wrecking havoc over our lives." I squeezed Gran's fingers within mine.

At that moment, Joey and Billy exploded out the door of the dock house.

"We're starving," Joey declared. Billy nodded in agreement.

"Okay, let's get moving," Gran said and slid on to her red scooter.

We followed Gran up the driveway to Rosebud with Joey and Billy running rings around us. My head was spinning by the time we made it to the back porch.

The next morning, Royce delivered our runabout. He told Mr. Wilkes that Rene was tied up with customers who wanted to discuss building a new boat for their company, then left, taking the borrowed boat back to the shop. It was wonderful to have our twenty-footer back. Now Mr. Wilkes and I could put out nets and bring in a mess of fish with room to spare.

As soon as Royce left, Mrs. Mayo walked through the dock gate. She was wearing one of her balloon dresses, splashed with blue hues that matched the color of the sky and a big floppy straw sunhat to shade her plump face from the harsh sunlight.

"Darling, I'm so glad I caught you before y'all began cleaning fish," Mrs. Mayo said. She eased her bulk down on the picnic bench, wiping sweat from her brow with a dainty white handkerchief that she held between pudgy little fingers.

"Hello, Mrs. Mayo, it's nice to see you. Would you like a Coke?" I asked, opening the cooler next to the picnic table.

"Why, thank you," she said, taking the can from me.

Mr. Wilkes went about preparing the dock equipment for cleaning fish, while I sat with Mrs. Mayo and had a Coke with her. She was all smiles and dimples as her hat fluttered about her face in the morning breeze. Deputy Jones and Clay Lyons had taken the day off, so I could relax without feeling their eyes upon me. It was bad enough Wilson, Rene's employee, was still in the dock house watching our security cameras.

"Lucy dear, I have a favor to ask," Mrs. Mayo said, her dimples flashing. "You know poor Mack Dykes and his family have been devastated by Sue Ann's death. I want to have a get-together for them at our restaurant. You know, all his friends and family — to show our support. Of course, Lucille, you, and Mr. Wilkes are invited. Y'all are Mack's best friends."

"That sounds wonderful. What can I do to help?" I asked.

"I want to have the get-together tomorrow night at my restaurant. Do you have enough fish in stock to feed a crowd of about fifty?" Her pudgy fingers were twisting the dainty handkerchief.

I calculated the fish we had in stock plus the possible bounty that awaited us tomorrow morning. "After Mr. Wilkes and I bring in our catch in the morning, we should have enough."

"That's wonderful! I'll send Mikey to pick up the fish tomorrow before lunch. Just add everything to our account." She tapped my cheek with her fingernail and floated through the dock gate, her balloon dress catching the breeze.

"I heard," Mr. Wilkes said, as I walked up to him, tying an apron over my jeans and T-shirt.

"Well, it's good money and we also get to go to the party. You can't beat that," I said with a chuckle.

"Rita will be excited about a party," Mr. Wilkes commented. "But I think the Dykes family needs a miracle to get Junior out of this, seeing how guilty he's been acting lately." He dumped a container of whole catfish, too small for filleting, but perfect for frying whole. I spent the best part of the morning cutting off fish heads and gutting their bellies. Sweat dripped down my face as the sun climbed higher overhead.

Mr. Wilkes filleted two forty-pound catfish, dropping their white bloody meat on the cleaning table. He dumped the fish guts into the barrel hanging beneath the cleaning table and then loaded it onto the runabout.

"I'll shoot this downriver while you clean the dock," Mr. Wilkes yelled back at me as he jumped into the runabout and took off. I sighed, grabbed the water hose and washed the dock clean, then scrapped the cleaning table free of slimy fish guts until the marina sparkled in the afternoon heat. I rang Gran to tell her about Mrs. Mayo's party.

"Come on up, lunch is ready," Gran ordered.

Man was I hungry for her macaroni and meatloaf.

CHAPTER TWENTY-SEVEN

FIREFLIES DANCED IN THE NIGHT air illuminating the back porch of Suzanne Mayo's restaurant as we pigged out on fried catfish, hushpuppies, and coleslaw. Everyone had dressed casually in jeans and cotton shirts. Mrs. Mayo's four sons were mingling about the room, flirting with any females who showed off too much cleavage. Three of the older sons were tall young men with a mane of thick dark red hair and sea-green eyes, which twinkled with merriment. Their Irish ancestry was evident. It came through their grandmother's side of the family, the Sullivans. The Mayo's were not far behind having come from Scotland at the turn of the nineteenth century. Then there was the youngest brother, Mikey, so short and chunky, with brown eyes and buckteeth, who took after his mother's short stature. His arms were muscled like tree trunks from manual labor. No young lady encouraged his attention. Mikey hung in the background, lighting his cigarette with a gold and silver lighter, too elegant for his use. His mother immediately extinguished the cigarette, reminding him of the smoking ban ordinance posted in all public restaurants in the city. Mikey stuffed his hands into his jean pockets and stomped down the backstairs of the porch and out into the night. God had played a nasty trick on Mikey. I felt sorry for him. Only seventeen years old, and he already carried a huge chip on his shoulder.

Junior and his father took center stage at a large round table, which held a *Lazy Suzy* turntable at the center offering endless samples of seafood and side dishes. I couldn't believe my eyes when Leah Ellis pulled up a chair next to Junior. She looked just as usual, a cool ash-blonde beauty. He seemed startled to see her, but quickly recovered and offered her a plate of food. Leah's large gray eyes ate him up. He blushed and quickly turned around in his seat to talk to his father. Junior's sons were inside playing racecars with Joey and the other children.

Gran circled my waist with her arm and we strolled down the porch steps toward the back garden. Stars devoured the sky with their universal secrets. Gran and I sat down on a wrought-iron garden bench and soaked up the night air whispering through the tree leaves.

"Suzanne did a good thing bringing everyone together tonight," Gran commented, taking my hand. I squeezed her fingers.

"Yes, she did. I feel like these past few weeks never happened," I said and then sighed deeply because I knew they had. Sheriff Ware was no closer to finding Sue Ann's killer than the day it happened. Sheriff Umbridge of Cope County was as much in the dark as everyone else.

"You know, I talked to Sheriff Umbridge at the co-op yesterday," Gran said, as if reading my mind. She squeezed my fingers in return. "He told me some interesting things about Sue Ann's investigation. They have a DNA sample of the killer's blood from the floorboard and his fingerprints left in her blood on the truck seat. It's only a matter of time, before they find him." Gran turned to face me. The moonlight caressed her skin, pale and soft like that of a newborn.

"That's good to know, Gran. But let's talk about something more cheerful, like how much fun the children are having inside right now." I didn't want to discuss Sue Ann's case out here in the garden. You never knew who was hiding in the darkness. Just then the bushes rustled nearby and Mr. Wilkes and Rita appeared, hand-in-hand, enjoying an evening stroll. He was wearing dark slacks and a cotton polo shirt — so un-Mr. Wilkes.

A band struck up shortly after ten o'clock and all married couples with children, gathered them up to leave the dance floor to the younger crowd. Gran and I found Joey as he was saying good-night to Mr. Mack's grandsons. Junior would remain behind for a little while longer, Mack said to Gran. I wondered if Leah Ellis had something to do with it.

"Lucille, I'm so glad you could come out tonight," Mr. Mack said, dropping an arm about Gran's shoulders.

"Wouldn't have missed it, Mack. Bring the boys around soon." Gran headed for the station wagon. Mr. Mack saw us off.

I stumbled over an object sticking out of the gravel. I leaned down and scooped up a gold and silver lighter engraved from top to bottom with the word *SAD* on the left side of the lighter. I turned to give the lighter to Mr. Mack, but he was already heading indoors. I thought back to Mickey using a similar lighter earlier this evening in the garden. Mikey's outlook on life reflected upon a lighter, so elegant, yet engraved with such a negative sentiment. I shook my head and slipped in behind the wheel of my Chevy truck. I'll return the lighter to Mikey next time I saw him.

"Mommy, you know what David told me?" My son sounded very solemn, before letting out a big yawn.

"What, honey?" I encouraged his seriousness.

"David says a lady with black hair and long red fingernails has been creeping around their house at night. He says she jingles like Santa's Christmas sleigh," he managed to finish before dropping off to sleep.

Startled, I looked over at Gran as she held Joey's head in her lap and she turned to look at me. The only one who fit that description was Jetta Angelo.

What in the hell was Jetta doing at Junior's place in the middle of the night?

CHAPTER TWENTY-EIGHT

JUG FISHING WAS A LOT like hanging clothes on a clothesline, but a little more hazardous. Mr. Wilkes and Clay were seated behind the console while I stood starboard, waiting to drop the first white jug strung with fifteen feet of nylon line. Sharp fish hooks were tied to the line every foot or so. I dug into the bait box at my feet and threaded a plump worm onto each hook before dropping the line into the water. Mr. Wilkes trimmed up the motor each time I dropped a hook, so that an hour later I had put out twenty jug lines just past the bend in the river. Clay kept an eye out for anyone who might show a little too much interest in my direction.

"We should have a mess of fish by late afternoon," Mr. Wilkes said, trimming down the motor as he took off toward the marina.

"Lucy, you handle the jug lines like a pro," Clay said, admiringly. Sunshades hid his eyes from me, but a sincere smile played about his lips.

Cricket and Clay had been seeing each other since the Grappling Event. I'd heard from the grapevine that Cricket was smitten.

"Thanks. Been doing it all my life," I said, but felt my lips twist into a grin.

The roar of an outboard motor came from around the bend and suddenly the red jet boat flew by — too close — causing our runabout to ride out the wash. Jetta Angelo was piloting the boat. She was clad in a bright pink bikini, her long black hair snaked out behind her in the wind. She gave me the finger and disappeared around the next turn.

I froze. My mind went back to Rene's pretend ignorance of the current owner of the jet boat.

Mr. Wilkes eyed me. "You want us to follow her?"

"No. I wouldn't give her the satisfaction." I stored the bait and then sat down cross-legged in front of the console, needing a moment of privacy without their eyes on my face. Rene had jerked me around twice now. His innocent remarks were becoming more and more demeaning. It was time to put distance between the two of us until he made up his mind about which woman he wanted to share his life.

The sun warmed me as Mr. Wilkes flew over the waves. Neither man said anything, respecting my need to think in silence. Joey waved from the marina as we made our final turn into the dock slip.

"Mommy, Mommy!" Joey ran up to the runabout. "David is coming to spend the night." He jumped up and down, his face full of smiles that lightened my mood.

"Good, honey," Stepping out of the runabout, I hugged Joey's warm body against me. Billy had gone home that morning to spend time with his brothers and sisters, so I knew Joey would greatly appreciate David's presence.

Later that morning, Junior arrived with David in tow. Mr. Mack had stayed behind to watch David's brothers. David was so like Junior, it brought back fond memories of us as children.

Mr. Wilkes began washing off the dock, cleaning up after dressing out fish earlier that morning. Clay helped him drop the fish crate back into the river.

"Junior, may I have a word, before you leave?" I asked. Mr. Wilkes gave me the evil-eye, but I ignored him. Sliding across the bench seat of the picnic table, I reached over and opened the cooler, pulling out two Cokes for us.

Junior sat next to me, accepting the Coke. "What's up?" he said. His mood seemed good, almost happy.

Just then, Gran called down to Joey, asking him to bring David up to the house. The boys chased each other up the hill, laughing whenever one tagged the other.

"Junior, are you seeing Jetta Angelo?" I asked, looking him straight in the eye.

Junior had the grace to blush He looked away, out over the river at the morning traffic.

"Jetta showed up the other night. Dad had taken the boys to get ice cream and I was alone watching television, wondering what-the-hell happened to my life. Jetta was like an exotic drink that you can't get enough of. I know it was wrong, so soon after Sue Ann's death, but we were in the bedroom before I could blink." He looked back at me. "How did you find out?"

"David saw her," I said in a stern voice.

"Jesus, I didn't know. He never said anything to me." Junior's eyebrows came together in a frown.

"He's seen her more than once," I reprimanded him.

"Oh, Lord, I'm crazy." Junior cradled his head on the picnic table. His muscular arms shook before I realized he was crying.

I felt like a heel, digging into his personal life. None of this was my business. Jetta was driving me crazy and it was all Rene's fault. The sudden realization that I was in love with Rene hit me in the gut. I was the green-eyed monster, taking it out on Junior.

"Listen, Junior, I'm sorry. I shouldn't have asked you about her," I said and stood up.

"No, it's okay." He grabbed my wrist, stopping me and wiped his eyes with a handkerchief from his back pocket. "I need to talk about it. Leah has been putting pressure on me to marry her. I guess it was my way of getting free of her, you know, by seeing Jetta. Now Jetta's putting the screws on me. What gives with these women? We're all too old to expect a marriage proposal just because we have sex." He was really in denial.

"Junior, a woman doesn't want to be used like a tool and then dropped," I scolded. "Making love is more than just a release for the woman. A woman interprets sex as giving a part of herself to someone she cares about. They don't want a *slam, bam, thank you ma'am.*"

"I never told Leah or Jetta that I wanted anything more than sex," he defended himself.

"Yeah, but what do you say to get them into bed?" I queried. I knew all the lies men say to trick a woman into giving them their bodies.

"Okay, Lucy, I know where this is leading — right back to college." He took my hand and kissed my fingers.

"No, you're wrong." I pulled my fingers from his grasp. "I'm trying to understand why a man who had everything, found it necessary to cheat on his wife."

"That's what I've been trying to figure out. I hate myself for wanting more than one woman. I lie awake at night knowing I drove Sue Ann to her death. But it didn't stop me from enjoying Jetta." He shrugged his shoulders.

"Junior, you're like a little boy who can't get enough candy. But you know, after a while your teeth rot from too much sugar, and no one will want you then." I slid off the picnic bench. This conversation was getting me nowhere. Junior would always be the same. There would be many Jetta-like women in his life.

"You gonna hold this against me?" he asked in a little boy's voice.

"You're a friend. I can't judge you." I made the mistake of looking at Mr. Wilkes. He definitely was not pleased at our conversation.

Late that afternoon, Mr. Wilkes, Clay, and I geared up to go back on the river to check the jug lines. Junior had departed earlier after spending time with Gran up at the house.

I thought about my feelings for Rene. I knew I would have to confront him with the knowledge that Jetta was driving the jet boat, and wondered what new lie he would tell to deceive me. I couldn't help the negative thoughts that came to mind. Since my first husband had let me down so miserably, it was hard to take a leap of faith.

I twisted my long hair into a braid and hunched down in the boat so I could lean over the side and snag the jug line with a grappling hook. Gently, I eased up the nylon line. A ten-pound catfish slapped water into my face as I swung him over the side of the boat and he flopped back and forth on the floor, trying to get free of the hook. I slipped on thick rubber gloves and took firm hold of the catfish, wrestled the hook from his lip, and tossed him into the live-well. We continued along the trail of jug lines, unhooking catfish, crappies, and buffaloes until we reached the last jug bobbing in the river. The river was peaceful here, no traffic or swimmers. The breeze had picked up and clouds were gathering to the west. A storm was brewing. I'd better hurry this up.

"Miss Lucy, we best get back," Mr. Wilkes said, reading my mind.

"These summer storms sure do develop quickly," Clay acknowledged. "Need some help there?"

"It's okay, I got it." I appreciated his offer, but I had a system and preferred to finish out the trail.

I shivered as the temperature seemed to drop a few degrees. I leaned over and slowly gathered the line, untangling the hooks from each other as I went. So far, no fish, I was disappointed. The last hook was heavy. *Man, it's got to be one hell of a fish*, I thought. A mass of black seaweed-type debris came to the surface. I looked over my shoulder at Mr. Wilkes, then went back to pulling on the line. Suddenly a white form appeared all wrapped in the nylon line. I drew in a shaky breath. Jetta Angelo's face was frozen in time. Her dark eyes held the secrets of the river and her pink bikini was twisted so that the top exposed her breasts. The nylon line was wrapped tight around her neck and it was impossible to simply slip it off. Sharp hooks dug into her flesh. Red talon fingernails captured the sun and mirrored its reflection. I made a mewing sound like a cat, and Clay was suddenly at my side, taking the line from my fingers. Mr. Wilkes wrapped his arms around my shoulders and dragged me back. I was in shock. I couldn't move, blink, or breathe. Mr. Wilkes said something to Clay, and the next thing I knew I was being wrapped into a blanket and they were forcing me to drink the contents of a white cup. I choked, coughing and coughing on the stiff whiskey they poured down my throat. God help me. I never wanted Jetta dead — just out of my life.

Later, I vaguely took note of Sheriff Ware coming on board. Mr. Wilkes and Clay carried me to the sheriff's boat and took me back to the marina. Gran put me to bed and I lay in the darkness of my room. I knew I would be the number-one suspect in Jetta's murder unless the mysterious Bubba made an appearance somewhere down the road.

CHAPTER TWENTY-NINE

EARLY THE NEXT MORNING, AFTER a hot shower and breakfast, I ran down the hill with Joey and David at my side. I felt suddenly carefree, like a weight had been lifted from my shoulders. Jetta had been a thorn in my side for some time now. She had interfered with Rene and me on several occasions, sometimes violently. Jetta's reign of terror over us had been complete.

Sheriff Ware showed up about thirty minutes later. I told him about the time Jetta showed up at Rene's apartment with a bloody bandage wrapped around her upper arm and divulged my suspicion that Jetta had piloted the boat, which disabled my runabout. I also said I suspected she had been the one who shot at Rene and me on our dock and that Rene knew, but hadn't told me because of their past relationship. Finally, I filled him in on how Jetta had endangered the Cub Scouts on our camp out.

"Miss DelRose, after going through Angelo's house earlier this morning, I would have to agree with your suspicions. She had pictures of you and Rene plastered all over her walls. She was obsessed with you. There were pictures of you disfigured and there were ones of you in a grave." I felt weak at the knees and suddenly swayed forward. Sheriff Ware leaned toward me, holding me upright.

I was glad we were sitting down at the picnic table. It looked like Rene had spoken the truth when he said he had broken up with Jetta — though — it still didn't excuse his trying to protect her by lying to me.

"Angelo was killed shortly after you witnessed her in the jet boat yesterday afternoon." Sheriff Ware continued. "She was strangled with the nylon line. The jug line was in an isolated spot near an abandoned campsite, so there were no witnesses. You and Rene were the only suspects I had up to this morning. But just as I drove up, I got a call," Sheriff Ware looked at me over his sunshades. "Junior Dykes just made the list."

"What!" It had never occurred to me that the sheriff would already know about Junior's relationship with Jetta. It had happened so recently.

"The jet boat she's been riding around in belongs to Dykes. He'd been loaning it to her the last few days while he was at work." The sunglasses rattled against the picnic table as the sheriff threw them down, causing me to jump.

"Oh, Junior, you just had to get involved with that gypsy woman," I moaned, covering my face with my hands. Junior had enough problems and this just added salt to an open wound. I remembered how happy he had looked yesterday — until — we discussed Jetta.

"It seems once this Angelo woman got a hold of a man, it became impossible for him to escape." The sheriff removed his felt hat to wipe the rim with one of our napkins.

"In that case, there may be other men she obsessed over that would want to get rid of her," I said, hopefully. I didn't want Rene or Junior involved in her killing. I was ashamed at how little faith I had in Rene. I'd been so ready to throw him under the bus that I would have ruined any chance of us having a future together. I'd never been so possessive about a man before. It was a scary situation.

"I'll have to question them both," the sheriff said, sliding his hat back on his head and slipping on the sunshades. "I'll get back to you as soon as the autopsy has been performed." He walked out the dock gate. I wish we could find Bubba and question him.

Mr. Wilkes and Clay had been cleaning fish that I had taken from the jug line yesterday. Clay was beginning to enjoy the activity.

I decided not to call Rene until after Sheriff Ware questioned him. I could still see Jetta's dark eyes staring up at the sky. Those golden bracelets she usually wore to announce herself would never jingle again. I wondered if Rene would miss her unannounced visits to his shop, but I knew I'd feel more secure knowing she could never stalk me again. I wondered if I should dismiss Clay, but something nagged at the back of my consciousness, so I decided to keep him on a few more days.

Around noon, Cricket Sykes dropped in on us to have lunch with Clay. Cricket's red hair and flashing green eyes had him spellbound.

"Lucy, I can't believe what happened to that gypsy woman," Cricket said. "It's all over the news."

"Surprised me, too," I acknowledged, taking a big bite of the chicken salad sandwich Gran had prepared.

Joey and David sat on the dock playing with toy trucks. Mr. Wilkes joined Gran and me at the picnic table. Clay and Cricket ate in the dock house. Life was good.

The roar of twin engines had us looking out over the river to see Rene's cabin cruiser coming in on its own wash. He tied up at the dock rail. Rene was wearing jean shorts and a blue T-shirt over his muscular frame and the wind tossed his black mane about his shoulders. Just watching him walk my way, I fell in love all over again. He walked like a jungle cat, so sure of himself. His bronze skin glowed.

Rene shook Mr. Wilkes' hand and nodded to Gran. He took my hand in his and kissed my fingers, one at a time. My heart did a flip.

"Rene, can I get you a sandwich," Gran asked.

"Thank you, Mrs. DelRose, but no. I've already had lunch." Rene slid in next to me at the picnic table. His body threw off a tremendous amount of heat.

"Well, then, I'll take the boys back up to the house," Gran said. She called to Joey and David to follow her, slid onto her red scooter, and headed up the driveway with the boys following. Mr. Wilkes washed his hands with the water hose.

"I'm sorry you were the one to find, Jetta," Rene said, pressing his lips against the palm of my hand.

"It was a shock," I admitted. I drew in a breath as his lips moved up my arm to the hollow at the base of my throat.

"When the sheriff told me how she obsessed over you, I wanted to wring my own neck," he said. "I should have seen how far she would go to get my attention." He took me into his arms and kissed me. All the knots in my back and shoulders unwound and I melted against him, letting his arms wrap around me.

"I've always felt her presence," I whispered against his mouth. "I'm sorry she's dead, but it has taken a load off."

Rene released my hair from the scrunchie, running his fingers through the blonde strands until the breeze stirred them to life. His fingers worked wonders as he stroked my shoulders. I turned my back to him and rested against his chest, enjoying the hardness of his body against mine.

"I'm very worried about the person who killed, Jetta," Rene said, dropping hot little kisses on my neck. "I want you to continue being careful. This person may have an agenda we know nothing about."

"I agree," I replied, breathless. "I'm keeping Clay on for awhile." My lower extremities were heating as Rene nibbled at my earlobe.

"I'll pick you up tonight around eight so we can go uptown for dinner. Wear something sexy," he whispered against my ear. His breath tickled.

"Okay," I whispered back.

"Leave Clay with Joey and your grandmother." Rene gave me one more kiss and then boarded his cruiser. He motored south toward his shop.

"I heard that," Cricket said with a wide grin. "Clay, it looks like our dinner date is out." She turned around and Clay walked up behind her.

"That's okay," Clay said, wrapping an arm around her waist. He kissed Cricket on the cheek. "It'll give you time to work on your next promotion. We'll go out tomorrow night if Deputy Jones can take my place." He looked at me and I gave him a thumps up.

The hall clock chimed eight times as I walked out the front door with Rene. I was surprised to see he was driving a silver Corvette. I'd never seen him in anything but a boat or truck. He opened the passenger door and I slid into the seat, careful not to show too much leg in my silky black dress. My legs appeared longer in black nylon hose. Rene closed the door and walked behind the Corvette before sliding in next to me.

"You know, you look good enough to eat," Rene said, running his fingers through my long blonde hair. His lips pressed against mine and I felt his hunger.

His hair was soft and he smelled so sexy. All I wanted was to get him into bed. Thinking about making love to him seemed so natural now. I couldn't imagine losing him.

We drove downtown to Fredrick's, a nice seafood restaurant with white tablecloths and real silverware and good china. Candles flickered about us and we were in a cocoon of romantic bliss. We ate lobster and drank white wine. A dessert cart was rolled over to us and I chose a rich chocolate pudding. Rene went with strawberries dipped in hot chocolate.

Two hours later, we strolled out of Frederick's like a honeymoon couple, and ran right into Mikey Mayo.

Mikey was two sheets to the wind. He stumbled into us, knocking me into Rene, who managed to keep his balance and catch me.

"Sorry, folks," Mikey blurted out, then hiccupped. His eyes looked bloodshot and his clothes were in disarray. He reeked of beer.

"Mayo, you okay?" Rene said, placing a hand on Mikey's shoulder to steady him.

"Right as rain, my mother would say," Mikey said, hiccupping.

"Where is your car?" Rene said, holding onto him.

"Last I saw, it was at home. I came here with a friend—." he said and started to sit down on the sidewalk.

"Look, let us take you home." Rene put his hand under Mikey's arm and pulled him back up.

"Miss Lucy, you look real fine tonight," Mikey said, and gave me another hiccup.

I tried not to laugh. "Thank you, Mikey," I said and looked away.

"Why can't I find a pretty woman like you to date?" Mikey tried to sit down on the sidewalk again, but Rene had a hand on the back of his shirt and hauled him back on his feet.

"Maybe if you didn't get so stinking drunk, you could find a nice girl to date," Rene said, steering him to the Corvette. He eased Mikey into the backseat and then came around and opened the door for me.

"I'd treat you real good, Miss Lucy," Mikey said, picking at a scab.

"Kid, the only thing you're going to do, is get home and sleep it off," Rene slid into his bucket seat.

The roar of the Corvette kept Mikey quiet until we pulled in his driveway. Mrs. Mayo peered at us through the front screen door as Rene left the car and walked up to the porch to tell her about Mikey.

"Hey, honey," Mikey addressed me. "I could pick you up sometime, you know, take you out." Then his eyelids closed and he dropped off to sleep.

I grinned. Teenagers were a trip.

Mrs. Mayo called out to her other sons, and they came and pulled a very drunk Mikey from the car and into the house.

Rene was laughing when he got back into the car.

"He's going to have one hell of a hangover tomorrow," he said, turning the key. The Corvette roared to life.

"I feel so sorry for him. I don't think he can get a date," I said.

"Then he's not trying very hard." Rene dropped the gearshift into third and we flew over the country roads on our way back to Bunge.

CHAPTER THIRTY

ARMORED CATFISH HAVE RUGGED scales along their backs and spiky fins, and they're black with white patterns running over their bodies like a crazy maze. This fish had to be the weirdest thing I'd seen since the alligator gar. Unfortunately, I had just stepped on an armored catfish that was burrowed into the side of the sandbar.

"Ouch," I said, clutching my foot and dancing around on one leg. Blood dripped from the pad of my foot.

Clay ran over to the runabout and pulled out the first-aid kit, then hurried back to me.

"You must have stepped on a shell." Clay wiped my foot with an antiseptic cloth before wrapping a bandage around it.

"No, it was an armored catfish. They have a hard shell-like body and sharp fins. This one was burrowing into the sand, probably laying eggs." I inspected Clay's handiwork.

Clay had come with me this morning to check out a sandbar about a half mile north of the marina. I hoped to use the site for a group of seniors who wanted to go fishing this evening, a group of ladies from one of Gran's club.

I hobbled back to the runabout. Clay shoved the boat back into the water and then jumped onboard. I trimmed down the motor, and we took off across the main channel, heading south toward the marina. I knew I shouldn't go barefoot, but it felt so good. Since spending time with Rene last night, my inhabitations were dissolving. Tonight, we were going riding in his cruiser. I licked my lips in anticipation.

Mikey was waiting for me at the marina when we pulled up to the dock slip. He was radiant in the morning heat. His red hair had been brushed into a wave, he was dressed in white shorts and a black muscle shirt, and he wore sunshades. I wasn't used to this new Mikey, and already I was sure that I was going to regret taking him home last night.

"Hey, Miss Lucy," Mikey came running up to us and put out his hand to help me from the boat.

"Thank you, Mikey," I said, stumbling slightly from the cut on my bare foot. Mikey caught me, pulling me close to him, and I could smell his strong cologne. Gently, I untangled myself.

"Clay, I need to go up to the house. Could you see to Mikey for me?" I gave Clay a *get rid of him* look, and Clay winked at me. I started toward the dock gate, Mikey made to follow, but Clay turned him toward the runabout.

"Hey, Mikey, need a hand here," Clay said.

I ran up the stone steps and into the house like the devil was after me.

"What's up?" Gran looked up from the newspaper.

I had told her about taking Mikey home last night. "Guess who's on the dock?"

"Who, dear?"

"Mikey — and he's here to court me. I think our being nice to him last night gave him the wrong impression." I gnawed at my lower lip.

"What happened to your foot?" Gran peered over her reading glasses to look down.

"Armored catfish dug into the sandbar." I wiggled my toes.

"Don't go barefoot. You always run into these complications," she reminded me.

"I know, I know," I muttered.

Peeking out the window, I saw Clay walking Mikey back to his truck, a blue Dodge Ram. Whew! Thank goodness for Clay, I thought. For some reason Mikey had made me uncomfortable.

Damn, I forgot to ask him about the gold and silver lighter.

Later that evening, Mr. Wilkes left to pilot the club ladies over to the sandbar to fish. Gran decided to join them. Since I would be going out with Rene on his cruiser, she took Joey with her. Deputy Jones, tackle box in hand, went along with Mr. Wilkes to protect Gran and Joey, and Clay had already left to pick up Cricket for their date. We all seemed like happy clams that evening. I liked this feeling of bliss. Sue Ann and Jetta were far from my mind. I just wanted one night with no worries.

I dressed in pink shorts and a white halter-top, leaving my hair to blow in the breeze. The river smelled clean as the traffic settled down for the night and the moon gave off a lunar glow while dusk settled around me. Crickets took up their active chirping and the fireflies lit their tails for my enjoyment. My cell phone buzzed in my pocket and I fished it out.

"Hello," I said, tossing my hair back over my shoulder.

"Hi, baby," Rene said softly in my ear.

"Where are you?" I was breathless with anticipation.

"I'm sorry, but I have to cancel our date. The government head official, Brian Meeks, arrived right at dark and wanted to go over some changes to the design on two of their boats. He's only here for tonight, and then he flies out at dawn." Rene didn't sound pleased.

"No problem," I said. "I'll grab an early dinner and wait for Gran and Joey to get back home from the sandbar." But the disappointment was contagious. We mumbled our good-byes.

I called Gran and told her I was in for the night, then latched the dock gate and walked up the stone steps at an even pace. The pain in my foot had subsided and the evening air lent a hint of mystery. I had just made it to the porch when Mikey appeared around the corner of the house, startling me.

"Lord, Mikey, what are you up to?" I said, pressing my hand to my chest.

"Just paying a call on you, Miss Lucy." Mikey was breathless with excitement. His eyes traveled my body. A chill went through me.

Wilson Woodson ran up from the dock house.

"Everything okay, Miss DelRose?" Wilson asked.

"Yes, thank you, Wilson. Mr. Mayo was just leaving. Could you please escort him to his truck? He must have parked out front somewhere." I edged toward the kitchen door.

"Be my pleasure, Miss DelRose," Wilson said. He began to hustle Mikey toward the front yard.

"But Miss Lucy, I just wanted to visit you awhile," Mikey whined, wrestling his arm from Wilson's grasp.

"Mikey, please go on home. I've got a ton of bookkeeping to work on." I stood by the doorway until Wilson put a hand on Mikey's back and directed him to his truck. Tires spun against the gravel when Mikey pulled out. Wilson came back shaking his head.

"What a character," he said with a smile.

"I know. He gives me the creeps." I gave an exaggerated shake of my body. Wilson laughed and headed back to the dock house to watch the security cameras. I was so relieved to have Wilson here tonight, but it made me miss Rene all the more.

Again I forgot to bring up the lighter. I think I'll just give it to Sheriff Ware and let him deal with Mikey.

I punched in the security code, in case Mikey showed up again, then I prepared a light dinner and settled in the living room to watch an old classic movie on television. Here I was humming with anticipation and no place to go.

Gran and Joey showed up about two hours later. Joey yawned his way to bed while Gran and I sat up, discussing Mikey's sudden attraction to me.

"Gran, I'm twelve years older than he is," I said. "What is he thinking?"

"That's the point, he isn't thinking. He's reacting to your looks." Gran patted my hair.

"But I've known him since he was small and he's never showed a bit of interest in me before," I said, exasperated.

"Ah, but he wasn't a teenager then. Boys at this age come into all those raging hormones. Just ignore him and he'll find someone else," Gran assured me.

"I hope you're right." I kissed her goodnight.

The next morning, Rene called and offered to take Joey and me four-wheel riding along the sandbar across the river. Knowing Joey's fondness for any all-terrain vehicle, I accepted.

"I'll pick y'all up right after lunch," he said. "Could you wear something that will show a little skin?" He all but purred into the receiver.

"Well, the four-wheeler might burn my legs," I hedged with a smile.

"No problem. I had leg guards put on, so you should be good to go." He laughed and disconnected.

Joey was excited and bugged me all morning while Mr. Wilkes and I cleaned fish. Gran prepared lunch and then joined Mr. Wilkes and Clay in the dock house to wait on customers. Since Rene would be with Joey and me, I wanted Clay to stay and watch over Gran. I knew Jetta was no longer a problem, but her killer might be. Sue Ann's murder now seemed so long ago that most folks had moved on to gossiping about more recent tragic events.

After lunch, Joey and I waited on the dock for Rene to pick us up in his cruiser. As instructed, I had dressed in white shorts with a matching tank-top. My hair was braided back from my face. Rene motored up from the south and tied up at our dock. As usual he radiated sexual vibes, showing off this time by wearing brief black swimming trunks with a matching short-sleeve nylon shirt. His black hair was wind-blown. His dark eyes twinkled at my unspoken assessment. Men!

Joey jumped up and down when Rene showed him the four-wheeler he was to ride. I was relieved to see it was small enough for a seven-year-old to handle.

Royce was at the wheel of the cruiser, a much older version of Rene, but still in the running with the ladies. He dropped anchor near the sandbar and helped Rene unload the four-wheelers, using a winch to lower them one at a time, onto a floating barge that then took us to the sandbar. Rene instructed Joey on how to use the controls, and we watched him navigate the sandbar's slippery slopes and wet spots before straddling our own four-wheelers. With a yelp of excitement, I took off at high speed, Joey followed me and Rene brought up the rear. The sand was like powder, so easy to travel. I did a wheelie going up a slope, but almost flipped over backward. After that, I slowed my pace, not wanting to encourage Joey.

We met up with another group of four-wheelers coming from the north and chased each other up and down the sandbar. One lone rider dressed in jeans and T-shirt, wearing a helmet began chasing Joey who squealed with delight. Then the rider started heading toward the water. Joey tried to angle away from the water's edge, but the lone rider cut him off and pressed forward, chasing Joey closer to the water.

"Joey!" I screamed. I dropped the four-wheeler into gear and shot off toward Joey.

Rene joined me.

I watched in horror as the sandbar caved in, taking Joey and the small four-wheeler with it. The lone rider whipped his vehicle around, heading north, and took off at high speed. I wanted to wring his neck, but first we had to get Joey out of that hole.

"Joey, can you hear me?" I screamed out at my son. But all I could hear was the revving of the vehicle down in a hole so deep that it was hard to see him. "Joey, can you hear me?" I call again. I heard crying from down in the hole and felt my chest tighten.

"Joey!" Rene boomed. "Answer me." Rene's voice was harsh with authority.

"Yeah, I can hear you," Joey yelled above the noise. Thank God, Joey was okay.

"Turn off the key," Rene yelled down to him.

"Okay," Joey said and then there was peace.

I hung over the sandy hole, and the sand shifted somewhat like quicksand. Rene pulled me back.

"We don't need two of you in there," he reprimanded me. I felt like a child, but I held my tongue. Joey was too important for me to be cross with Rene right now.

"Joey, I'm going to get a rope to haul you out of there. Don't move, or the sand will shift," Rene yelled down to Joey. A crowd of other four-wheel riders had gathered.

"Okay, Rene," my brave boy yelled back. Rene took off on his four-wheeler back toward the boat. Joey's head was barely visible in the dark hole. My knees began to shake. Just then the sand shifted and Joey dropped a few inches. He screamed out, alarmed.

"Honey, I'm here. It's okay, Rene's getting the rope." I wanted to hold him in my arms while I beat the shit out of the rider who'd driven him onto the weak sandbar. I heard Rene's four-wheeler heading back toward us. Royce was with him.

Rene and Royce worked together to loop the end of the rope, weighing it down with a small anchor and Rene eased the rope into the hole.

"Joey, you'll see the rope dangling in front of you," he called down. I crawled closer so that I could watch. The rope went taut. Joey must have reached out and grabbed it. Just then, the sand gave way again. I screamed and flung my arms down into the hole, reaching for Joey. Royce caught me before I fell in. Tears flowed and everything blurred. Then I heard Joey's voice close to my ear. Wiping my eyes on my halter-top, I saw my son climb out of that damned hole and I reached for him. We clung together, rolling away from the danger. The crowd clapped their hands, relieved at my son's rescue.

I kissed his sandy face until he giggled.

"I'm okay, Mommy," he kept saying, trying to reassure me.

Rene and Royce spent some time trying to hook a rope to the small vehicle, before Royce went back to the boat to retrieve a grappling hook and they finally pulled it out. By then, both of them were covered in sand. Rene took Joey's hand and calmly walked into the river to wash the sand off. Royce just shook himself and was satisfied.

"Does anyone know who that rider was who chased, Joey?" I asked the crowd that had gathered.

"We saw the guy come over the levy from the Louisiana side earlier," answered a teenager in red swimming trucks, "but he didn't get close enough for us to see his face."

"I saw him unload the four-wheeler from his truck," a girl called out from the back of the crowd. She moved forward.

"What kind of truck was it?" Rene asked her.

She practically fainted from his attention.

"I think it was a Dodge, no, maybe a Chevrolet," she said, all boney knees and freckles. "I have a hard time telling trucks apart, but I know it was dark blue."

"Did you get a look at his face?" I asked, still clinging to Joey.

"Yes, ma'am," she said, making me feel like an old school teacher. "I remember noticing he had copper color hair, before putting on the helmet. He wasn't very tall, about my age," she added, addressing Rene.

"Did you talk to him?" Rene asked, giving her all his attention. Her mouth dropped open.

"No, he got on his vehicle too fast and headed away from us."

Another girl came forward and took the freckled-face girl by the arm.

"Thank you," Rene said and then hauled Joey up over his head and settled him on his shoulders behind his head. "Come on, kiddo, I guess you deserve some fried fish and hush puppies." Rene tickled Joey until he screamed with laughter. How easy it is for children to cast off terrifying situations and return to normalcy. But I couldn't forget that someone had tried to hurt Joey just for the hell of it.

CHAPTER THIRTY-ONE

A COPPER HAIRED TEENAGER, DRIVING *a Dodge truck*. That's what the young girl had said yesterday after Rene rescued Joey from the sand pit. She could have been describing Mikey Mayo, for God's sake, I thought, slamming the lid of the empty crate box. I must be going out of my mind. Why would Mikey, of all people, want to hurt Joey? And how did Mikey know we would be at the sandbar yesterday at that exact time? I pushed the button on the crane to lower the crate back into the Mississippi River. Mr. Wilkes and I had to run nets after supper.

"Lucy, supper's ready. You and Mr. Wilkes come on up," Gran yelled down to us from the porch. I didn't know why she just didn't call us on her cell phone. Old habits die hard, I guess. I motioned to Mr. Wilkes, who was standing over by the picnic table talking with Wilson.

"You go on up, Miss Lucy," Mr. Wilkes said, and gestured with his arm. "Wilson's telling me something."

I nodded and headed up to Rosebud. Deputy Jones was off today so Clay would ride with us this evening when we ran the nets. It looked like we were making a fisherman out of Clay.

A few hours later, the sun bathed us in a warm glow while we loaded the runabout with life preservers, grappling hooks, extra nets, and five gallon buckets. After gaining entrance to the main channel, Mr. Wilkes piloted the boat south, navigating the muddy water, and then angled toward the Louisiana bank, taking a backwater channel between hanging mosses to a secret lake. Bird calls echoed in the jungle of trees surrounding us. The bull frogs' throaty conversations blanketed us with the serenity of the moment.

Clay helped me pull up the nets and empty catfish and crappies onto the floor of the runabout. The last net held a surprise — a thirty-pound catfish with a soccer ball wedged into its mouth. The poor thing was struggling mightily so to get the ball out. Clay and Mr. Wilkes fought the withering catfish for some time, trying to help, until suddenly I had an idea. Reaching over, I pushed in the ball's stem to let out the air. Finally the ball was loose enough for Clay to pull it from the fish's mouth. We took pity on the catfish and dropped him overboard. He had suffered enough for one day. The catfish flicked his tail at us and disappeared beneath the water. All in all, we had had a good haul. Clay and I started separating the fish into live-wells so it would be easier pulling them out in the morning.

We cleared the secret lake and motored into Louisiana waters, heading to the main channel, which was full of Mississippians having fun. Ahead of us about a quarter of a mile or so, bikini-clad women waved at passersby from the deck of a crowded ski boat. Closing the distance, we saw to our horror the pilot falling to the floor, releasing his control of the ski boat. It veered to the left, heading straight for a barge parked along the Louisiana bank. The women began to scream, running about wildly, trying to grab the steering wheel. One of them fell out of the boat and landed belly-up in the river. The ski boat struck the barge with powerful force, throwing two more women into the water along with some of the ski boat's men. The boat started to climb onto the barge, but lost traction when the prop became entangled in the anchor chain, stalling the motor.

"We've got to help them," I cried out. Mr. Wilkes was already heading toward the bodies floating in the water. The first woman didn't look too good, but when Clay threw out a lifesaving floater, she grabbed for it. He pulled her in and wrapped her bruised body with a blanket from our first-aid compartment.

"Thank — thank you," she managed, coughing up water.

Clay gave her a sip of whiskey and she coughed some more.

We coasted in toward the barge, along with the other boaters who had come to help. The men had been pulled out of the water by one of the dock workers. I was startled to recognize Leah Ellis among the women who'd been rescued. Her usual cool demeanor was absent, marred by the tragedy of her mates. I knew one of the men to be dead from the way the boaters pulled him from the water. His eyes were glazed over and his mouth was slack. But the shocker came minutes later as Mr. Wilkes piloted closer to the refinery boat. The dead man was Ricky Downs, the hippie from the Blue Bird Bar & Grill. The pilot was nowhere to be found.

Leah's rescuers transferred her to our boat since they were headed north away from the boat landing. The woman we'd picked up turned out to be a clerk from Junior's co-op.

"Where is, Bubba?" Leah screamed out. "I saw him go into the water." She pointed to the front of the barge.

Bubba! Finally I am hearing the name that has haunted me since Junior took me to the Blue Bird Bar & Grill.

The refinery boat and two others joined in the search for Bubba's body. The sheriff's boat arrived minutes later and Sheriff Ware boarded our runabout to talk to the two witnesses.

"Miss Ellis, what happened?" Sheriff Ware sat on the upper deck, looking down at the bikini-clad women. The woman Clay had pulled out of the river had toweled off her hair, and it was beginning to dry, revealing strands of red.

"Bubba was driving his ski boat and the next thing, he was on the floor, and the boat crashed into the barge." Leah was crying, clinging to the redhead.

"Who is this, Bubba?" the sheriff asked.

"Bubba Simmons," hiccupped Leah's redheaded friend.

"Was he drinking alcohol?" the sheriff said, writing on his notepad.

"We all were drinking, Sheriff," Leah said, as if he had insulted Bubba.

"Who does Bubba Simmons work for?" the sheriff said.

"Old man Bryers still has his air-conditioning business," the redhead volunteered. "He keeps Bubba around in case some of his old customers call."

"I know Mr. Bryers," Sheriff Ware said. "Has Simmons been working with him a long time?" The sheriff tipped back his gray-felt hat.

"Some years now," Leah said. "He comes over to the farm co-op off and on to pick up supplies."

Bingo! I looked at Mr. Wilkes and he nodded. We finally had Bubba's connection to Sue Ann and our final clue to the mystery of Ricky Downs's telephone call the night Junior and I had visited the Blue Bird Bar & Grill. Ricky Downs surely had known about Bubba's activities and I guessed it had gotten him killed. So far, Bubba's body had not surfaced in the muddy waters around the barge. I suddenly jumped to my feet, an idea came to me.

"Mr. Wilkes, can you get me close to the barge please? I want to check out something." I climbed the ladder to the upper deck, ready to jump onto the barge.

"Where you go, I go," Clay said, following me.

"Okay, Miss Lucy, it's as close as I can get," Mr. Wilkes, yelled out.

"I'm coming too." Sheriff Ware joined us on the deck and we jumped onto the barge one at a time.

I walked across to the side that was resting close to the river's bank. There, as plain as day, were footprints leading from the water's edge and disappearing into the woods. I turned to see if my cohorts had noticed, too.

"I'll be damned," Clay said, giving me a pat on the back.

"I'll call the sheriff over in Delhi and get him to start looking for our Mr. Simmons," Sheriff Ware said. "He's got a lot of explaining to do."

When we got back into the runabout, I whispered to Mr. Wilkes at what we found.

"What's going on?" asked the redhead.

"Miss — ?" The sheriff raised an eyebrow in her direction.

"Mrs. Rose Cross," she said with a sniff from her runny nose.

"Mrs. Cross, Ricky Downs is dead," Sheriff Ware told her. "I need you and Miss Ellis to stop by the station in the morning and give me your statements about what happened today." That ended their questions. Clay helped the sheriff's deputies transfer the women to the sheriff's boat.

"All this time and Junior didn't connect Bubba Simmons to Sue Ann?" I said.

"Maybe he didn't know Bubba," Clay said, with a shrug.

"Simmons has been in the co-op as much as Miss Leah said, Mr. Junior would have known him," Mr. Wilkes said. "My guess is his real name isn't Bubba." He gave us a knowing look.

"You could be right." I gave him a smile, then called Sheriff Ware on my cell and relayed out suspicions about Bubba, including his name. The sheriff said he would get back to me. So much for our final clue.

Now, what could Bubba Simmons be up to?

CHAPTER THIRTY-TWO

THE NEXT MORNING, I SAT on the back porch, swinging back and forth on the porch swing. Deputy Jones sat in the wicker chair next to me. "Lucy," Gran called out, "could you pick up David at the co-op? Joey wants a playmate."

"Okay, Gran," I called back reluctantly. At the moment I wasn't keen on speaking to Leah or Junior.

"Sheriff Ware said the Simmons man's full name was Harry Robert Simmons," Deputy Jones told me. "Mr. Bryers started calling him Bubba and it stuck. He's a real loner. The only friend Mr. Bryers knew was the dead guy, Ricky Downs. Seems Simmons and Downs were involved in drugs. Simmons was arrested twice for drug possession in Louisiana, but never did any jail time, but Downs did two years in Cope County a while back. The sheriff believes Mrs. Dykes bought the marijuana that the medical examiner found in her system at the autopsy from one of them."

"Here's a picture of Simmons." Deputy Jones showed me a mug shot of a gaunt man with stringy shoulder-length hair. He wore horn-rim glasses and sported a goatee. "You may need this to identify him, if he starts following you for some reason." Deputy Jones stood up, hat in hand.

"I wonder if Sue Ann was killed by one of them," I said as I rose from the swing, gathering my purse and keys to pick up David. We decided that Deputy Jones would go with me while Clay stayed with Gran.

"Be careful, you two," Clay said. He was dressed in kakis with a holstered .38 at his side.

"Don't worry about us," Deputy Jones said. "Just take care of things here."

We made it to Junior's co-op about an hour later after stopping for Cokes and snacks along the way. The green farmland whisked by as I pushed down the gas pedal, hitting seventy miles an hour.

"Now, Miss Lucy, you need to keep it under fifty-five," Deputy Jones scolded me. "The sign is posted fifty-five, and I'd hate for you to get a ticket."

Feeling remorse, I eased up on the gas pedal and cruised sixty miles an hour all the way to Rolling Fork. Junior's co-op sat back from the road in an old mill store, two huge silos flanking its side. We parked and went indoors. Leah was seated in her office, but most of her usual luster was gone. She was taking Ricky Downs' death pretty hard. Or was it Bubba's disappearance that worried her? I swore to keep my nose out of it and asked for Junior.

"He's somewhere in the back loading seed bags," she said dully, her eyes on the documents in her hand.

"Thank you," I said and angled toward the back doors with Deputy Jones on my heels.

David's excited voice vibrated off the walls along with the chain motors of feed bags being unloaded. David saw us right away and hurried over.

"Dad's in his office," David said. "Let me tell him I'm going with you." He was acting so grown-up since his mother's death.

"Okay, honey. We'll wait here." I leaned against the dirty seed bags, not caring if my jeans got dusty. Deputy Jones, on the other hand, kept to the middle of the room, obviously wanting to keep her uniform clean.

Junior came out of his office, dirty from head to toe, but his face was more relaxed than I'd seen it in some time.

"Thanks for coming all this way, Lucy. Hello Deputy Jones." Junior put out his hand and the deputy reluctantly accepted his handshake.

"If you want David to spend the night, let me know," I said. Slipping an arm around the boy's shoulders, I began herding him to the front of the store.

"I'll let you know." Junior leaned over and hugged me, to Deputy Jones' disapproving stare. I gave her an *I don't want to hurt his feelings* look and she returned it with *you'll never learn*. Oh, well, I could live with that.

We arrived back at Rosebud an hour and a half later, after stopping off at the local Sonic Restaurant. David had to have an ice cream cone.

Joey ran out and hugged David, then they hurried off to Joey's room, where they played video games the rest of the day.

About an hour later, Rene motored up to the dock. Mr. Wilkes and I were cleaning the fish we'd caught yesterday while Clay scooped them from the live-well with a net. Rene jumped down from his cruiser and rushed over to me.

"I heard about Simmons and Downs from the sheriff a while ago. Why didn't you call me?" Rene said accusingly. He knelt down on his hunches next to me. He was sexy as hell, even when he was pissed.

"Rene, so much has been happening, I can't catch my breath," I said. "I'm worried about Bubba Simmons and the role he played in Sue Ann's death. Now he's disappeared, I have to keep bodyguards, just in case." I laid down my knife.

"I'm sorry, baby. I didn't mean to upset you," he said. "I worry about you twenty-four hours a day," Rene gathered me close. I hated smelling like a fish, but enjoyed the scent of him. His lips tasted good when he pressed them against mine.

"Tomorrow I'll take all of you to Natchez for a day trip," he said with an enticing smile.

"I accept!" I said, excited. "I've wanted to revisit Natchez for months now." I kissed him back.

"We'll eat lunch on the boat and have dinner in town." Rene gave me a final kiss before heading back to his boat. Waving good-bye, he pilot south into the main channel.

I felt on top of the world. The whole family spending the day together.... This sounded promising.

"You are one lucky woman, Miss Lucy," Mr. Wilkes said, slapping down a chunk of catfish meat for me to clean. "Mr. Rene is courting you, taking your family about town like that."

"I know, isn't it wonderful." I couldn't stop grinning.

Mr. Wilkes shook his head. "You've got it real bad, Miss Lucy." Grinning, he gave me the last of the catfish meat.

"You make it sound like the flu," I teased.

"At least with love, you don't have to take something to get over it," he said with a chuckle.

Dear Mr. Wilkes. I continued to smile.

It was clear blue skies when Rene tied up his cruiser early the next morning. Against Gran's wishes, he loaded her red scooter onto the boat deck.

"Now, Mrs. DelRose, you know Natchez is full of hills. I don't want you tiring yourself." Rene was firm. Gran didn't say another word.

Joey and David jumped on board. Junior had agreed to let David stay an extra day. I had packed extra clothes and snacks. I wore a light blue sundress and leather sandals. Gran's sundress was of mint-green with clovers. Rene wore knee-length cargo shorts and a cotton short-sleeve shirt. We looked like a married couple taking out our two boys and their grandmother for a day in the sun.

The trip to Natchez took a little over two hours. We passed several tugboats along the way, and the boys waved and pulled the chain to toot the horn. The tugboat pilots always returned their greetings.

"Rene, do you think some day I could pilot this boat?" Joey asked, his eyes glowing with anticipation.

"You can count on it, Joey," Rene promised. Joey danced back to David with a thumbs-up.

"Rene, your cruiser rides like a dream," Gran complimented him.

"Mrs. DelRose, I spend a great deal of time on this cruiser. I want her to run as smooth as glass." He patted the steering wheel. Gran laid her hand over Rene's and gave it a squeeze.

We anchored for a lunch of cold sandwiches and some of Gran's favorite orange and pineapple cake. We were still licking our fingers when Rene started the motors and continued downriver.

As we approached Natchez, the bridge that connected it to Vidalia, Louisiana came to view in the distance. A quaint old town nestled against a hill that led to the Mississippi River, within the last few years, Natchez had increased its revenue by allowing casino boats to operate along its riverfront. We tied off at a new docking station and jumped down from the boat. Rene used a ramp to unload Gran's red scooter. Gran boarded the scooter and we all went uphill to the small shops that lined the river walk, entering an air-conditioned antique store with an array of eighteenth- and nineteenth-century marbled tables and prism candelabras. There were dainty china dishes and silver serving ware. I enjoyed looking at everything. Finally, the boys became restless and wanted to run around, so we left the store.

David and Joey dashed up and down the wooden sidewalk until they were hot and breathless. We stopped at a small yellow trailer serving Italian shaved ice and sat down to eat our way through soft ice coated with cherry juice until we all had red lips and tongues. I stuck out my tongue at Rene and he surprised me by leaning forward and licking mine with his. I drew in my breath, turning away. The brute chuckled softly. Gran ignored us.

A green and red tourist trolley stopped at the loading dock and we boarded her. Rene stored Gran's scooter in a baggage bin. The trolley's interior was a woodsman's dream with paneled walls and varnished bench seats. Joey and David sat together behind the driver. We settled Gran across the aisle from the boys and then made ourselves cozy behind Gran.

The trolley went past several antebellum homes before stopping at Melrose Plantation, where the passengers could tour the inside of the white columned house. The extensive lawn and gardens were impressive as the trolley pulled into the gravel driveway, circling the side lawn; past Southern live oaks draped with Spanish moss, and came around to the backdoor of Melrose. Gran was giddy as a schoolgirl when Rene helped her board the red scooter. We followed the other tourists up to the bookstore that housed memorabilia and information about Melrose. Park rangers arranged for us to tour the mansion in groups of ten. We ended up in the second group, which would start in thirty minutes.

"Come on, Gran. Let's check out the gardens," I encourage her.

"Good idea, Lucy." Gran maneuvered the red scooter down a small grassy hill to an old black iron fence.

"What lovely iron lace," she said, caressing the ironwork.

"Here, Mrs. DelRose, let me open the gate for you." Rene leaned over to raise the latch and swung the gate wide.

We passed through history as we made our way down to the gardens, the circular driveway where once horse buggies would have dropped off visitors still intact. I sat down on the stone steps soaking up the atmosphere. Crepe myrtles were heavy with blooms. Wisteria bushes blanketed the lawn in a carpet of purple.

"Mommy," Joey whispered. "Are there ghosts here with us?" My wide-eyed son looked about expectantly. David's eyes opened wider.

"Yes, honey. I feel their presence." A tickle of wind passed over me, lifting my hair and cooling my heated skin in the wet humidity.

"I would like to see the old oak trees," Gran said, and off she went into the menagerie of droopy limbs.

We hurried to catch up to her and ran smack into a tall, thin man with long stringy hair, sporting a goatee and wearing horn-rimmed glasses. I gasped, recognizing Bubba Simmons in the flesh.

"Excuse me," he mumbled and scurried off toward Melrose.

"Rene, it's Bubba Simmons!" I turned to him anxiously.

"Okay, y'all stay here. I'm going to follow him." Rene said. He took off after Simmons. "Call Sheriff Ware!" he yelled over his shoulder.

I fished in my back pocket for my cell phone and dialed the sheriff's number.

"Sheriff, we've got Bubba Simmons," I began, excited.

"Where?" the sheriff said.

"Here in Natchez, at the Melrose Plantation. Rene is following him." I turned to see if I could catch a glimpse of Rene.

"I'll call the Natchez sheriff's department and we'll be there as soon as possible. He could be dangerous." Ware warned. "We're charging him with vehicular manslaughter in the death of Ricky Downs." The sheriff disconnected.

"Okay, y'all, let's head over to the front entrance of Melrose and wait for Rene." I helped Gran turn the scooter around. Joey and David fell in step beside us.

Suddenly Bubba Simmons crashed through the wisteria bushes and body slammed me onto the ground. Rene burst through after him and we all ended in a tangled mess, arms and legs intertwined like an old twister game.

Rene and Bubba were breathing heavily, but Rene managed to press his knee into Bubba's back. I scrambled to my feet, shielding Joey and David from Simmons.

"Get off me, man!" Bubba screamed out, thrashing about on the grass. "I haven't done anything to you."

A lady dressed in a park ranger's uniform hurried towards us from the main driveway of Melrose.

"What is going on here?" she said, huffing and puffing, her bulky weight hindering her ability to catch her breath.

"Sheriff Ware of Bunge County has a warrant out for this man, charging him with vehicular manslaughter," I chimed up in Rene's defense.

"Well, I'm the law here at Melrose, and you will let him go," she said, cheeks still red from exertion.

"I don't mean to step on your toes, ma'am, but we are making a citizen's arrest until the sheriff gets here," Rene said with authority.

The park ranger drew a .38 automatic from her hip holster and pointed the pistol at Rene's head.

"I said let him up," she threatened, her finger on the trigger.

It was at that moment I noticed her name tag, *Martha Simmons*. Lord, help us.

"Ms. Simmons, isn't it?" I purred. "I don't appreciate your drawing your weapon in front of my son and his friend."

"Are you related to this man?" Rene barked at her.

"He's my nephew, if you must know." She stiffened her stance, refusing to be intimidated by Rene.

"If you don't mind, I'm going to take my son, his friend, and my grandmother to the front of Melrose and wait for law enforcement to arrive," I said."Don't do anything that may jeopardize you job, Ms. Simmons. From what I know about your nephew, he's not worth it." I turned away, urging Gran, Joey, and David through the blue Spanish moss, leaving Rene to deal with the park ranger how he saw fit.

The Natchez sheriff and two deputies arrived within five minutes.

"Sheriff Renfro with Natchez County, ma'am." The sheriff held out his hand to me and I shook it.

"I'm Lucy DelRose, and this is my grandmother, Lucille DelRose, our friend, David, and my son, Joey," I said, waving to each in turn.

"Sheriff Ware tells me you've spotted Harry Simmons," the sheriff said, looking about.

"He's behind the oak trees." I pointed to my left. "A friend of ours, Rene Caron, captured Harry Simmons and made a citizen's arrest. But Simmons' aunt is the park ranger here and she's holding a gun on Rene." I sat down on the brick steps that led to the massive oak doors of Melrose. Joey and David leaned against me, tired. Gran fanned herself with a brochure to ward off the heat.

"Thank you, ma'am." The sheriff and his team disappeared through the wisteria, shaking the purple blossoms to the grassy lawn.

"Can you believe running into Simmons when we were having such a good time?" Gran complained.

"It seems to be my norm," I said. I'd begun to accept that it seemed my fate to appear where there was trouble.

Sheriff Renfro soon returned, leading a group of hot, miserable people through a narrow opening in the Spanish moss. The plants seemed to caress their heads as they pass beneath. Rene was talking with the sheriff. Park ranger Simmons no longer possessed her firearm, and she looked really pissed. Harry Simmons was handcuffed. The two deputies led him across the lawn.

"We want to thank you, Mr. Caron," Sheriff Renfro said, shaking Rene's hand. "Your Sheriff Ware is flying in by helicopter from Bunge County."

Harry Simmons looked at me with hatred and I stepped back, alarmed.

"Just couldn't keep your nose out of this, could you!" Simmons yelled at me. The deputy tightened his hold on Simmons.

"I don't know what the hell you're talking about. You killed Ricky Downs, not me." I stood my ground.

"I'm not talking about that pathetic loser. I'm talking about Sue Ann's old man. You helping him out, trying to find out her killer. Who do you think you are, Sherlock Holmes?" he said with disdain.

"Well, I'm not wearing handcuffs and you are," I retorted, equally disdainful.

"I'll get you back for hurting my aunt. She'll lose her job because of you." He spit on the ground in front of me.

"No, asshole, *you* lost her job. You disgust me, coming here and hiding behind your aunt's position as a park ranger. Take your punishment like a man." I stepped back. I had no interest in someone who thought of life as one merry-go-round of handouts. "Besides, you probably killed Sue Ann." I couldn't help myself. I had to get one more dig in.

Simmons went ballistic and made a lung for me. The Natchez deputies subdued him.

"I did not kill that bitch!" Simmons yelled. "She was doing some teenage kid. He's the one who killed her, not me!"

I was instantly reminded of the gold and silver lighter I found at the Mayo Restaurant with the word *SAD* engraved upon it. By god! It wasn't a word, the engraving were initials for Sue Ann Dykes! Mikey Mayo and Sue Ann Dykes? Impossible!

Suddenly we heard a whirling sound, and all looked up. There, by God, was a helicopter hovering above the lawn of Melrose Plantation. Slowly the helicopter descended until it touched down. The copter door opened and Sheriff Ware and Deputy Griggs stepped out, heading toward us. The helicopter's long blades kept up a continual sweeping motion, stirring up the heat.

Joey and David were no longer tired. They jumped about, wanting to get closer to the helicopter, but Rene held them back.

"Well, Miss DelRose, as usual you are on top of things," Sheriff Ware said, shaking my hand. His skin was smooth and cold from the air-conditioner inside the copter.

"We literally ran right into him, sheriff," I said with a shrug. "I had no plans of tracking him down."

"You are a magnet for attracting bad guys," he said, then looked at Rene with a smile.

"I plan to do something about that pretty soon," Rene replied, grinning. He gave me a wink.

I blushed and then turned away to help Gran to maneuver her scooter around a broken brick on the walkway while Ware and Renfro exchanged pleasantries.

I pulled the sheriff aside and told him about the gold and silver lighter.

"Do you have it on you?" he asked.

"No, it's back at the dock house," I said.

"I'll drop by later and pick it up," Sheriff Ware said.

"See you then," I said, shaking his hand.

"I'm taking Simmons back to Bunge for booking. See all of you later." The sheriff tipped his hat to us and then the Bunge group boarded the copter and took off in one dusty swoop. I tried brushing blades of grass from my clothes, but it didn't seem to make much of a difference. I really needed a bath.

Park ranger Simmons was taken into custody by Sheriff Renfro for aiding and abiding a suspect in a crime. She wasn't happy, but I did try to warn her.

We ended up cutting our trip short. Rene ordered a private bus to take us back to his cruiser, then called to order dinner from a seafood restaurant along the river walk and had it delivered to us on board. Rene was turning out to be a man of many surprises. I smiled my gratitude at his thoughtfulness.

CHAPTER THIRTY-THREE

HARRY SIMMONS WAS CHARGED WITH vehicular manslaughter in the death of Ricky Downs. After several hours of interrogation, Sheriff Ware determined Simmons had no connection to Sue Ann's murder. Simmons never met Jetta Angelo and had no idea who killed her. He was held on a $250,000.00 bond.

"Sheriff Ware, what does Junior do now about Sue Ann?" Gran asked as she poured tea into his glass.

"If Mrs. Dykes was keeping company with a teenage boy, she did a good job of hiding it," Sheriff Ware said. "But Simmons said every time he sold her marijuana, she told him she was in a hurry because she was meeting someone."

"I'm surprised you're not charging him with selling drugs," I said, taking another bite of my sandwich. I needed a break from cleaning fish and had invited the sheriff to lunch when he'd showed up. Mr. Wilkes had elected to stay at the dock house and have a sandwich with Wilson in the security room that doubled for our stockroom. Clay had a doctor's appointment and would be back after lunch.

"We made a deal," Sheriff Ware said. "If he confessed to vehicular manslaughter, then we'd drop the drug charges. He accepted." The sheriff took a bite of his sandwich.

"What a world we live in," Gran said. "Commit two crimes and get away with only being charged for one. No wonder crime is so out of control in this country." She finished her sandwich and went to check on Joey and David.

"Lord, I almost forgot — here," I said, handing the sheriff the gold and silver lighter with Sue Ann Dykes initials. I explained how I found the lighter and about Mikey lighting his cigarette with it earlier that evening.

"Good. I hope to get a fingerprint off the flint cylinder," he said. "But first, I need Junior to identify the lighter as belonging to Sue Ann. This one item may be the evidence we need to break the case wide open, and then we can get a court order to compare his DNA and his fingerprints left at the scene of the crime."

I nodded. Sheriff Ware slipped the lighter into an evidence bag and wrote information across it with his pen.

Yesterday's excitement with Simmons had put Gran in an uneasy mood. She constantly checked on Joey and David — every thirty minutes or so. It had affected me, too, making me realized that I needed to break clean from Sue Ann and Jetta. My family had always meant everything to me. I didn't want to take chances with their safety. Plus, Rene was talking serious commitment and my knees were knocking.

"I need to get back to the dock. Customers will start arriving soon." I threw down my napkin and cleaned the table. Gran had said she'd stay in the house with the boys. As soon as Sheriff Ware took off in his patrol car, I ran down the back stone steps to the dock gate.

Customers kept us busy until four o'clock that afternoon. Mr. Wilkes hosed down the dock, and Clay was helping me lower the crate back into the river when my cell phone vibrated.

"Yes," I said.

"Lucy, could you bring David to me?" It was Junior. His voice sounded strained.

"Sure, Junior," I agreed, wondering what was causing him to sound so odd.

"Listen, take your runabout and I'll meet you upriver near the casino," he said.

I heard a scuffle, then a grunt.

"Junior, are you okay?" I was becoming alarmed.

"Ah, yes, sorry," he said. "I dropped a hammer on my foot. I'll meet you in about an hour upriver. Okay?" He attempted a lighter mood. But I was not fooled. Junior was up to something again, still trying to discover who killed Sue Ann.

I would deliver David, I told myself firmly, and not get further involved with Junior's problems.

"I'll meet you in about an hour," I agreed and disconnected.

"What's going on?" Clay said, throwing an apron over the dock rail.

"Junior wants me to deliver David on the river in about an hour," I rolled up the hose and placed it on its usual rack.

"I'm going with you," Clay said.

"Okay. Just let me get David ready to go." I ran up the steps and told Gran the plan.

"Oh, Lucy, I don't like this arrangement. It doesn't sound like Junior at all," she fretted.

"I know. Clay's coming with me." I knocked on Joey's door and went inside.

Joey wanted to go with us, but I refused. My gut told me something was off with this delivery.

"Get the popcorn ready and I'll watch a movie with you when I get back. Okay?" I kissed Joey's head, feeling his soft hair.

"Oh, all right," Joey finally gave in.

"Thank you, dear," I said with a smile. David told him good-bye and went with me down the steps. The sky was darkening and a storm was moving in from the north.

"Let's get this over with before all hell breaks loose," Clay whispered to me.

We boarded the *Little Mermaid,* I insisted everyone put on a lifejacket, and then flipped the switch to lower the boat into the water. I trimmed down the motor and headed upriver. Traffic was light and the sky was darkening. Choppy waves began to slap against the hull as the wind picked up. I didn't like this. I was starting to turn back when I spotted the red and silver jet boat on the other side of the old Mississippi River Bridge. I pierced the underbelly of the iron bridge and pulled up alongside Junior's boat. When the figure at the wheel turned toward me, I was surprised.

Mikey Mayo pulled out a .22 pistol and aimed it at me.

Mikey Mayo *was* the teenage boy Sue Ann had been involved with. Mikey had tried to move on to me since losing Sue Ann.

"Don't do anything crazy. I have Junior tied up at a secret location. Lucy, you and David jump into the boat — now," he said forcefully. We all stood with open-mouths. I snapped out of shock when I realized Mikey was fool enough to think I would actually endanger David.

"Listen to me, you little bastard, I will not put do what you say." Out of the corner of my eye, I saw that Clay had slipped his .38 out of his holster, aiming it at Junior's boat. Before Mikey had noticed, Clay shot two holes in the boat below water level. The waves had become rough, and the boat began to take on water.

Mikey screamed and started shooting. I threw David to the bottom of the boat and hurled myself upon him. Clay returned fire and Mikey took a round in the shoulder, but managed to get off one more shot. Clay fell forward. I trimmed down the motor and took off across the river, heading south. Mikey gave chase. David lay on the floor crying.

Clay was bleeding from his leg. I rode the waves as rain tore into us, blinding me, then whipped the runabout around and headed straight at

Mikey. He panicked and turned the wheel too sharply. The jet boat flipped over, showing the belly of the hull and Mikey went sailing head first into the water. I stopped the runabout and threw out a lifesaver for Mikey. He made a grab for it, missed, and went under. *God, help me*, I prayed and dove into the choppy water to save him. I was glad I'd put on the lifejacket.

Mikey fought me at first, so I punched him in the face. Doing a side crawl, I flipped him over onto his back, cupped his chin, and made it back to the runabout. Clay leaned over and grabbed Mikey by his shirt, hauling him in. I swam to the stern and climbed up the diving ladder to the deck of our boat.

Clay whipped out his handcuffs and cuffed Mikey to the handrails. Then we made a tourniquet to tie around the gunshot wound in Mikey's shoulder and another tourniquet for Clay where Mikey had shot him in the upper thigh. David was a great helper. He didn't understand what had happened, but he didn't forget that his father was in trouble.

"Lucy, where's my dad?" he asked, clutching my shirt. I looked down at his face, wet from the rain, and knew we had to find out what Mikey had done with Junior.

Clay read my mind. He slapped Mikey on the face over and over until Mikey opened his eyes with a groan.

"Where did you leave Junior Dykes?" Clay demanded.

I put my hands over David's ears trying to shut out the words that would follow from Mikey and Clay.

"Sue Ann and I loved each other," Mikey sobbed. "She was through with him. Said all he did was run around on her. Then all of a sudden, she was ashamed of our love, said people wouldn't understand. She said I was too young. I begged her not to leave me, but she was dead set on it. I loved her so much I couldn't let her go back to him. I couldn't." Mikey choked on his own tears. "She made me do it. She made me kill her. I'm not sorry. I'm not sorry." He continued to sob.

Looking over at Clay, I decided to head back to our marina and get Sheriff Ware involved. Clay and Mikey needed their gun shot wounds attended to as soon as possible. I released David's head and turned toward the console.

Just then, my cell phone rang.

"Hello," I shouted over the storm.

"Lucy, where the hell are you?" Rene yelled frantically in my ear.

"Heading home," I answered him.

"Is Junior with you?" he thundered.

"No, as a matter of fact, Mikey kidnapped Junior and won't tell us where he stashed him. Mikey and Clay have been shot. David and I are bringing them back to the marina. Could you call Sheriff Ware for me? I kind of got my hands full here." I was running out of steam. David clung to me.

"I'll meet you at your house," Rene said and disconnected.

By the time we made it back to the marina, the storm clouds had begun moving off to the south. Mr. Wilkes was waiting for us on the dock next to our slip. I floated in on the choppy waves and trimmed up the prop, then cut the motor and threw the rope over to Mr. Wilkes so he could tie us off.

"Miss Lucy, you're a real piece of work, you are. Never a dull moment." Mr. Wilkes shook his head. He helped Clay take the cuffs off Mikey and they lifted him from the runabout and dragged him into the dock house and Clay sat down on the bench next to him wincing in pain.

"I called an ambulance to take both of you to the hospital," Mr. Wilkes said.

David still clung to me.

"Where's my daddy?" he asked again.

I looked over at Clay. He pulled out his .38 and pressed the barrel against Mikey's head. I quickly took David outside.

Mr. Wilkes left the dock house and joined us just as I heard the sirens approaching the house.

"Mikey says Junior's at some old campsite across from the Port at Bunge. He didn't give the exact location." Mr. Wilkes shrugged.

"I know where it is," I said in excitement. "Junior thought Sue Ann went there..." I stopped short, not wanting David to hear about his mother. Junior had been right from the beginning about the campsite.

Rene motored in on his cruiser. He tied it off and crossed the dock in four long strides. His arms crushed me to him and I hung onto to him, knowing how close we had all come to drowning in the storm.

"Rene, we need to go rescue Junior," I said, looking up at him. "David is very worried about his daddy," I added, knowing how Rene felt about Junior.

"Where is he?" Rene growled.

"Come on, I'll show you." I took Rene and David each by the hand. "Tell Sheriff Ware we'll be back shortly," I called out to Mr. Wilkes. He nodded and waved us off.

We got underway. Rene offered us cold drinks. David gulped his down. Glad to have something to do with my hands, I sipped my Coke. I told Rene where Junior was being held, and he motored upriver toward the old campsite. I also told him about Sue Ann's lighter.

"So, Mikey killed Sue Ann?" Rene whispered into my ear. David had sat down on the soft cushioned seats and had promptly fallen asleep.

"Mikey confessed." I leaned into Rene and his arms tightened possessively around me. "I'm not sure why he kidnapped Junior, or why he wanted me and David," I whispered back.

"I think maybe Mikey was falling for you and wanted to make sure Junior was out of the running," he said huskily into my ear.

We anchored the cruiser a few yards from the sandbar on the Louisiana bank.

"Stay here with David." Rene said. "I'll go and get Junior. You two have had enough excitement for one night." He leaned down and gave me a warm kiss.

"Okay, but be careful," I urged. "We still don't know who killed Jetta."

Rene jumped overboard and swam to the sandbar. I watched as he disappeared into the dark woods of an old trail leading to the camp.

After some time I heard a gunshot. I bolted upright. Why was their shooting? I thought this was just a rescue.

I pulled out my cell and called Sheriff Ware. He answered on the first ring. I brought him up to date and the sheriff said he was on his way. The call made me feel better, but I was still worried. Turned on Rene's spotlight, I slowly panned the sandbar, but didn't see any movement. The stars appeared as the last of the clouds floated south. A half-moon gave off a soft glow, kicking up a frothy trail of white along the shoreline of the bank.

Suddenly another shot rang out. What the hell was going on? Someone besides Junior had to be at the campsite. Mikey must have a partner working with him.

Just then, the sheriff's patrol boat dropped anchor next to us.

"Sheriff, two shots so far," I called out across the water. "I'm worried that Mikey had a partner."

The sheriff nodded. Accompanied by Deputy Griggs, he stepped into a small dingy and started the engine, taking off toward the sandbar. Frustrated, I watched the two figures disappear into the woods. Then a wisp of a figure ran from the darkness and dived into the water swimming out to the boats. I put on the spotlight and watched as Leah Ellis climbed out of the water and into the sheriff's boat. I couldn't have been more surprised.

"Leah, what are you doing here?" I shouted out. At first, she ignored me, then finally turned around.

"What do you have that I don't?" she yelled, her skin pale in the moonlight.

"What do you mean?" I yelled back.

"Rene wants you. Junior wants you and now Mikey wants you. When you said no to Junior, he goes after that slut Jetta Angelo. Well, I took care of Jetta and I'll take care of you." She laughed hysterically and started the motor, trimmed down the prop and ran the boat straight at Rene's cruiser. I grabbed a rifle from Rene's cabin and aimed it at her. I squeezed off a shot, striking the console. She abruptly turned the boat into the main channel, going north toward the Port of Bunge.

The woman was mad, crazy, confessing to killing Jetta. Was it true? Where were the men? Surely she hadn't killed them? Just as I thought about jumping overboard to find out for myself, the guys appeared in the clearing. I counted them off: Sheriff Ware, Deputy Griggs, Junior, and my darling Rene. God bless you.

I began crying and went to sit beside little David, who was moaning from all the noise.

CHAPTER THIRTY-FOUR

RENE AND I SAT AT the picnic table under the umbrella enjoying a new day. Gran and Joey were still in bed. Mr. Wilkes was in the dock house. I no longer needed Wilson, Clay, or Deputy Jones.

"I can't believe Mikey Mayo killed Sue Ann," I said for the tenth time since Sheriff Ware had confirmed last night. "He said Mikey's thumbprint was on the lighter's flint cylinder and they got a match on his DNA and fingerprints in Sue Ann's truck. Junior identified the lighter as Sue Ann's. He gave it to her on their wedding anniversary a couple of years ago."

"Mikey had been having an affair with Sue Ann, but when she wanted to end it, he killed her." Rene said. "The sheriff said Leah Ellis crashed the patrol boat into a barge throwing her into the water, breaking her neck."

"I feel terrible about Leah. All those plans she had made for her and Junior. Plans that Junior had no intention of keeping," I said. "Junior went after Jetta instead. Leah hated Junior for what he did to her, so she killed Jetta." I shook my head. "What a mess people make of their lives."

Just then, Joey clambered along the dock to sit next to me.

"Mommy, is Rene staying with us today?" He cuddled closer to me.

"Joey, how would you like it if all of us lived together for always?" Rene said, looking down at me. I held my breath.

"Oh boy, oh boy, I'd love it!" he yelled, jumping off the bench and doing a little dance on the dock.

"Rene…" I gulped, running out of words, my heartbeat pounding against my chest.

Rene pulled a black velvet box from his pocket and handed it to me.

"Lucy, I love you," he said with passion. "Please marry me and put me out of my misery." He kissed me hard, and then kissed me gentle.

"Rene, I've been waiting for you to ask me," I whispered against his lips.

Rene opened the black box and an oval diamond ring captured the morning rays within its prism and winked at me. I began crying, the ring was so beautiful. By giving it to me, Rene answered all my unspoken questions.

Rene slipped the ring on my finger and I held out my left hand, watching the various colors dance before my eyes. Then he pulled me onto his lap and nuzzled my neck.

"You still haven't answered my question," he teased.

"Yes, yes, yes, a thousand times yes," I purred into his ear. He gave my backside a gentle slap, grabbed the nape of my neck and kissed me until I thought I'd faint.

"What's going on here?" Joey asked, hands on his hips, looking at us.

"Do you want to be the ring bearer at our wedding?" Rene asked him.

"What does a ring bearer do?" Joey asked. Either way, he knew something exciting was about to happen.

"His job is to make sure the couple has their wedding rings so everyone will know they are husband and wife." Rene squeezed me closer.

"I can do that." Joey jumped up and down some more.

"Good. It's about time I put my brand on your mother," Rene said possessively. "That way other guys will know she belongs to me."

"Hey, she belongs to me, too." My son stamped his foot declaring his stake in this arrangement.

"I guess I can live with that." Rene reached over and grabbed Joey, tickling him all over. Joey shrieked with laughter.

My cell phone vibrated.

"Hello," I said, my thumb hooked to the side of my jean pocket.

"Lunch is ready," Gran said. "Y'all get on up here."

I laughed. Gran finally joined the twenty-first century.

THE END

www.ingramcontent.com/pod-product-compliance
Lightning Source LLC
Chambersburg PA
CBHW031337170626
46807CB00002B/743